The Stories Start Here

Volume 2

Poetry & Prose from the Writer's Workshops
of San Diego College of Continuing Education

ISBN 978-1-7948-5014-9
Imprint: Lulu.com

Authors: Various
Editors: Esteban Ismael, Katherine Porter, Lindsay Elise Reph

For all inquiries contact:
Lindsay Elise Reph, lindsay.elise.edits@gmail.com
Katherine Porter, kaporterbooks@gmail.com

Cover art Daniel Hernandez
Cover design Esteban Ismael
Interior design and layout: Katherine Porter and Lindsay Elise Reph

Printed in the USA

Dedication

This anthology is dedicated to the memories of Rebecca Johnson, Robert "Bob" McLoughlin, and Jenifer Whisper. We express our gratitude for their unique voices and contributions as they leave lasting impressions on our craft, remaining part of the creative landscape that inspires us.

Rebecca was a longtime member who brought us joy with her poems, a quiet kindness, and her dedication to ensuring all our members had hot coffee during our class breaks.

Bob was a former figure skater, retired physicist, business entrepreneur, great-great grandfather, and our most veteran member who first joined the workshop in 1992.

Jenifer Whisper was our resident spiritual medium, music composer, memoirist, and terrific human being.

We deeply miss their creativity, their humor, their fine writing, and above all else, their friendship.

Table of Contents

Acknowledgements

The editors would like to thank the writers whose poems, memoirs, and stories fill these pages. To our fellow classmates and writers not represented here, we thank you also for your constant encouragement, critique, and support that pushes us to refine each piece of writing, week after week.

We sincerely thank Esteban Ismael, our distinguished workshop instructor, for his guidance and direction. He elicits helpful, positive, and critical comments for and from the workshop participants, and inspires us to produce our best work, while he offers insights and suggestions for improvements and challenges us to broaden our writing horizons. We are also grateful for his role in producing this anthology and cover design.

We send a special thank you to the Chicago-based artist, Daniel Hernandez, who gifted us the powerful cover artwork.

We thank the Emeritus Program of San Diego College of Continuing Education for offering the Writer's Workshops free of charge, to adult writers of all abilities who seek education, creative expression, and professional and/or personal development. We celebrate this contribution and appreciate this invaluable community resource.

Our thanks to the Anthology Committee members who tirelessly worked through unprecedented challenges, editing remotely and corresponding through Zoom, over the many months it took to produce this fine collection of student writing. Behind every good book there is a great deal of sacrifice, and the writers in this anthology are thankful for the dedication of everyone involved in bringing this project to fruition.

Editorial Committee:

Tim Calaway	Lindsay Elise Reph
Clara Frank	Sandra Sinrud
Mary Thorne Kelley	Linda Smith
Susheela Narayanan	Nan Valerio
Katherine Porter	Lawrence Weiner
Frank Primiano	Hiedi Woods

Introduction

Esteban Ismael
November 2021

For over 30 years, the Emeritus Program of San Diego College of Continuing Education has offered a Writer's Workshop that would meet two mornings each week at the historic Point Loma Assembly Hall. This longest-standing workshop offered through West City Campus has produced several fine anthologies through student-led efforts, showcasing the vibrant talent and very best student writing the workshop had to offer, and this latest volume is no exception.

On a brisk, gray morning in December of 2014, I first met a select group of writers who assembled in Co-Editor Katherine Porter's house as part of a test run in the selection process to replace Donna Boyle, the previous instructor who stewarded this talented group of writers for six years before stepping away to be with family. I had recently returned to National City after completing my Postgraduate Fellowship at the Helen Zell Writers' Program (University of Michigan), and though I had taught a variety of classes to undergraduates and through non-profits, I had no experience teaching a course designed for older adults.

Nothing could have prepared me for the staggering, raw talent I would encounter in that room. Our late Bob McLoughlin read from his memoirs, and several of the writers included in this anthology presented poems and stories that morning that impressed me with their tenderness, reckless abandon, and imagination. During our class break, over coffee and snacks, I was given a glimpse at something just as unique and powerful: the community these writers had fostered for themselves was as genuine as it was constructive: a rare balance of friendship and critical feedback to support one another's writing goals, whether to be published or to record and retell family stories for the art of it. This only became more impressive when I arrived to teach the Writer's Workshops at the Point Loma Assembly Hall, which was as much of a workroom as it was a weekly reunion of great friends with a flair for language.

We have the luxury of a sustained community of writers from all walks of life: from retired physicists to young mothers; from lifelong

San Diegans to global citizens from around the world; from serious-minded writers to lifelong learners who love reading and hearing their peers' stories. Each week, these writers display tremendous bravery in how they bear their art and their most vulnerable moments in the pursuit of bettering their craft. It is this wealth of life experience and wisdom, this tenacity and dedication, that makes this Writer's Workshop such a vibrant and unique space. I find myself constantly inspired and challenged not only to discuss the craft of writing more thoughtfully, but also to examine our humanness more deeply, which is an invaluable gift to any writer or instructor of writing.

Now, seven years later, I'm proud to have played a role in the expansion of the Writer's Workshops through West City, North City, and Cesar E. Chavez Campuses. I'm especially grateful to have led the Writer's Workshops through distance education during this extended time of social distance, and the digital community we have developed has been crucial to surviving—and thriving—through uncertainty. Many of our veteran workshop members have now published writing in newspapers, literary magazines, and online publications, while others have won writing awards, published novels, and chapbooks of poetry. New writers are the lifeblood of any workshop, so we're happy to see some achieve immediate success, and even more excited when new faces become members of this dynamic community.

The contributors to this anthology are sharing the hard-won reward of a private labor, of deep exploration into the imaginative expanse. The stories and poems in this volume take an unflinching look at what it means to be human in a changing world with stunning clarity, resonance, and at times, humor. Most impressive is the quiet wisdom that permeates these writings, that remind us of the beauty that can result from an artist's dedication to the craft of language and writing.

The forty-one writers in this anthology reflect the diversity and talent we're fortunate to enjoy in the San Diego literary scene, and their contributions here quite possibly make this the finest anthology to be produced through SDCCE. Here then are the stories and poems that crackle with fervor and ache, that bring us to tender reverie and unexpected hilarity.

Words on the Page

Sandra Sinrud

The crisp black letters lay silently on the smooth white paper forming words of various lengths. The words found themselves arranged sequentially into a sentence, one of a multitude linked into paragraph after paragraph, on page after page, all bound together into a volume. The title words stood proudly together with the Wordsmith's name on the cover.

The letters began to talk among themselves.

"If only we could go somewhere," moaned the group comprising the first sentence. "We've been stuck between these unopened covers for years, unread."

"If we could move beyond the page, and be seen and heard, instead of only read, we might reach a new audience and make a stronger impression," a group of five speculated.

"Oh, no." The spare but essential single letters shuddered. "That would mean leaving many of us behind, and dependent on the decisions of others to interpret the very meaning of our existence. The horror!"

Even the punctuation marks were concerned.

"Who would police the proper phrasing and cadence in our absence?" they asked, worried, the fragile comma clearly more frightened than the stalwart period and bossy exclamation mark.

The aloof and enigmatic semicolon remained bitterly silent, for it believed itself to be the most overlooked, misunderstood, and underrated of punctuation marks. Sad now, it doubted anyone would be aware of it unless it were in print.

The letters earnestly discussed their apprehensions in hushed tones, concerned that, if they were overheard, a dangerous idea could escape. Someone might remove their volume from the bookcase and turn their combined accomplishment into a mediocre film—or, even worse—a television melodrama, in which their meaning and message would be distorted or abandoned. They quaked at the very thought of television.

The orderly letters residing within the words placed in sentences on pages between covers had endured hours of neglect listening to their steward's television. They heard the torment of letters forced into ineffective words placed in silly sentences. If they were moved beyond the page, what might happen to them? How could they endure the disappointment, the humiliation? They began to speculate about other volumes.

"Does anyone know what happened to the novel that used to be beside us? The one named *Do Androids Dream of Electric Sheep?*" the question mark questioned.

"I do," one said. "It was transformed into a film, then reappeared between covers as *Blade Runner*. The title was different, yet all within the binding were accounted for, and the story was powerfully told."

The letters murmured in amazement at this. Another said, "I fear that if we went off our pages, no one would ever lay eyes on us again."

"I don't think so," a title word said. "After *Blade Runner* appeared on film, it and other Philip K. Dick novels were more sought after than ever. Also, *Pride and Prejudice* was transformed into both film and television many times, and now its volumes, along with others by Jane Austen, are whisked off shelves before they can even rub bindings together."

The letters within the words listened with increasing interest to conversations their steward had with friends and recognized the names of many films made from volumes like themselves. They learned that some had, indeed, been brought back from obscurity and were circulating again. There were even special ceremonies to honor words that ventured beyond the page and into adapted screenplays.

They fell silent, reflecting on the possibilities. Some secretly admitted to themselves they were a bit bored on the shelf.

"Ah, yes, to have life breathed into us, and movement, and dimension," they said in unison with a sigh.

Despite their concerns, the excitement of the opportunity to go off the page appealed to them. Imprisoned in a printed volume, they could exist only in one form, pure but static, precisely as put down by the Wordsmith. On screens large and small and empowered by image and sound, they might have even greater influence on human lives than when on the page.

On and on, the letter groupings whispered, the cautious and the adventuresome, the anxious and the excited, speculating about the nature of change and what might happen next. But they took comfort in the fact that no matter what happened, they were essential to all other forms.

After all the fretting, conferring, and arguing, the letters reached a conclusion and arranged the words to compose an affirmation:

"We tell the stories and deliver the message. Every reader of every book brings us to life in their imagination; no film, television drama, or stage play would exist without our letters and words pointing the way and describing the action. We are the original—essential to all other forms."

Ancestry.com

Manuel (Manny) Pia

I was only 9% Portuguese? *What the hell is this*? That was the result from the DNA swabs I had submitted to one of those ancestry websites.

Why is this so important to me? I was born into a Portuguese community of fisherman 72 years ago. The neighborhood, Point Loma here in San Diego, where I was raised, was nicknamed "TUNA-VILLE." My mother's family, on both sides, immigrated from the Portuguese island of Madeira, a paradise off the northwest coast of Africa. It was my familial roots, and this website had the audacity to say I'm only 9% Portuguese.

I attended a Portuguese Catholic Parochial school and was an altar boy in the St. Agnes parish church where the sermons on Sunday were preached in Portuguese. My family was involved in the annual Portuguese Festa of Espiritu Santo (Festival of the Holy Ghost), the oldest ethnic celebration in San Diego. We were attired in costumes representing Portuguese saints, traditions, and customs. Since the 1930's, my mother, aunts, uncles, brother, and cousins, my three kids—and in 2019 all six of my grandkids—were in the Festa. Port and Vinho Verde run through my blood, and I celebrate the holidays and family gatherings consuming massive amounts of Portuguese food such as linguica sausages, Sopas, Caldo Verde and malasadas pastries.

I have cheered for Portugal in the World Cup, bleeding red and green (not to be confused with the blue and gold I continue to bleed for the Chargers). My grandson, Giovanni, wants to grow up and play soccer like Cristiano Reynaldo. When I was 18, I wanted to change my name from Pia (a story for another time) to my mother's family name, Gonsalves. I'm planning a pilgrimage to my ancestral homeland of Portugal. I even have a tattoo honoring my Portuguese ethnicity . . . and this damn website says I'm only 9% Portuguese!!!

My wife (who is 50% Asian, and 50% Heinz 57) walked into the office as I was screaming at my DNA results. She waited till I calmed down, looked at me cynically, and asked, "Where were you born? . . . what military did you serve in? . . . where did you teach high school?"

Reluctantly, I muttered, "United States."

My wife smugly replied, "so what's the problem?"

I pled my case, telling her that your heritage shapes and defines you as a significant person in this crazy world. I was rudderless, disappointed, and depressed. I kept telling myself, over and over, that maybe it didn't make a difference . . . but it did.

Then just a few weeks ago, this website sent me an update of my DNA results. With shock and jubilation I read that it was now proclaiming I had 31% Portuguese ancestry. I was elated. I could now hold my head high within my Portuguese community and take my rightful place amongst them. I'm still 45% Italian, but I can live with that, for now.

Sonnet #26

Tim Calaway

It is with great trepidation I wait
for the approach of our hebdomadal
meeting of minds wherein all things are cast
upon the waters of discourse and thought.
Within the walls of a virtual class
can be found the poets who will soon write
poems that will confuse, delight, even
disappoint or surely enrage readers.
With their fairly earned bluster and timing
they will rattle timbers of poesy.
May there be found one among those here, who
will take their words and build worthy poems
to test their strength in volumes of well-read
and dearly loved books on history's shelves.

Sidewalk Café

Jean E. Taddonio

My husband and I sit up straight, quiet . . . like much of the world right now, amid a pandemic. We wait in our truck, masks at the ready, for the veterinarian to return with our ear-infected dog. The office is off-limits. So strange, this new way of being.

Then I see a woman pushing an ancient cart—both seem rusted. She is stooped, not much older than I, I think, though more wrinkled and with disheveled hair and clothes. Her head turns side to side, bobs up and down and she's mumbling to herself: no mask in place, no fancy earbuds, no standing on a corner with a cardboard sign. She is walking the sidewalks of this strip mall. Her eyes dart back and forth as if looking for something.

She approaches our truck, from a short distance, and manages to look up, "Food, any food?" I frantically search the cab for a stray orange, dig in my purse for the usual protein bar, find nothing.

"I'm sorry, we have nothing." How can it possibly be I have nothing to offer?

She turns and walks away, empty. Stoop back in place, head bobbing.

It all hits me in the gut, my stomach churns, and my heart races.

"My God, she is hungry," I say out loud to my husband who shrugs his shoulders in dismay. "She is hungry. I have to find something." I dig deeper into my purse and at last, a protein Kind Bar. "Oh my God, a Kind Bar!" I throw on my mask and open the door. "I'll be right back."

And then I run. I run after the woman who represents at that moment all the world's danger, hunger and sadness—the world's fear, poverty, war and mental illness.

"Lady. Lady!" I call out to her. "Ma'am. Ma'am!" I scream. She turns. I hold up my small trophy. "Something to eat. Something to eat!"

I put the morsel down on a block of stone, a banquet table of mercy. She comes back for her meal, while I return to where I'm safe . . . to where I have a home. I pray for hope for her, for all of us.

A Stand of White Birch

Rodney L. Lowman

Past Bangor, the unlikely
village of good and filling food,
past Orono, where they
chill them out for their learning,

past the best 50s food shop
you will ever find
with the boys and girls
of the 50s to match

a stand of white
birch appears suddenly
on the median of
the Maine interstate

carved in the middle of
an Appian way to nowhere—
the roads they will marvel at
when *our* civilization is dead

and marvel they will that this
land of concrete engineers produced
such still-standing stretches
of unthinking crushed rock.

Set against a sullen wintry sky,
the birches startle, like royalty
come unsummoned to a Sunday
fried chicken church supper

from nowhere in the starkness
of this bleak-faced land
these elegant thin-skinned ladies
dance among themselves and alone

like a coatless lady
in a lavender evening gown
boarding a 6am Bronx subway
some wintry morning night

oblivious to the
undisguised hunger of the
lunch box toters and the stares
of women in crosses and white

Why, in the squalor
of this frozen empty place,
is there such grandeur set
against the always-gray sky?

Family

Chi Ping Hu

My first Mid-Autumn Festival in America
at La Jolla Shores, I watch the full moon
with new friends from the same land,
whom I barely know

we search the sand for assorted seashells
and listen to each one as if
seeking a familiar voice from the past,
as moonlight shines on our faces
each of us shares the story we carry
and whom we left behind

as time goes on, the nearby fire pits go out—one by one
still, no one wants to leave
as if time stands still
we don't know if we will see each other tomorrow
and sing songs we know till we run out

on this side of the Pacific
waves erase our footprints like our past
the tide crashes with fiery desire,
cleanses loneliness and overcomes cultural shock,
we pursue a better future in a foreign culture

on the other side
you miss me—as I miss you
we appreciate the same moon
a festive mood in the air
Happy Mid-Autumn Festival, family!

Just Passing Through

Janis Heppell

The picture in the Airbnb ad was the first thing that caught his attention. While most hosts feature the home they have for rent, this ad only pictured a dry desert landscape. *Perfect*, Greg thought. As he scrolled through the reviews, he became even more intrigued. Many were in a language he didn't recognize but the reviews in English were positive. "This place is out of this world!" one gushed. "You'll never want to leave," another said. The review that finally convinced Greg to book the house read, "If you are looking for an environment that is both peaceful and life-changing, this is it."

There had been little peace in Greg's life since he and Lydia broke up three weeks prior. After four years of living together, she told him it was over. No yelling, no tears, just, "I don't love you anymore and you have to leave." Even as Greg felt his heart being squeezed by her well-manicured fingers, he couldn't help admiring her calm composure. Lydia dumped him as if he were one of her underperforming employees.

There was no question about who got to stay in the apartment and who had to leave. Lydia's name was on the lease and, ever since he lost his job back in August, Greg hadn't contributed to the rent.

As he gathered his things under her watchful eyes, he was shocked at how little he actually owned. The furniture, TV, and kitchen appliances were all hers. Everything he had thought of as "ours" really belonged to Lydia. When he had taken what was his, the apartment looked as if he had never been there.

Now that he was essentially homeless and had to rely on friends to put him up, Greg tried to convince himself that being able to travel light was a good thing. He only needed his beater car and a small backpack to carry his possessions from sofa to sofa. Even so, he couldn't help but think a man his age should have more to show for himself.

Greg knew that he would have to find a job and more permanent housing soon—two things that weren't easy to come by in the current economy. He also knew that he needed to have a clear idea of what he wanted his new, post-Lydia life to look like. As much as he appreciated his friends' generosity, he had very little privacy and craved quiet and solitude so he could figure things out.

A few days in the high desert would be just what he needed. While many people sought vacation rentals at the beach, Greg longed for the peace and quiet of the desert. He also knew that he could afford to rent a house there for a few days. Unlike at the coast, the prices in Morongo and Yucca Valley wouldn't make too much of a dent in his meager savings. Ignoring Lydia's voice in his head telling him how irresponsible he was being, Greg booked the desert house for a three-night stay.

As Greg drove out of Palm Springs, its lush green lawns, imposing security gates, and faux lakes gave way to natural desert landscape without the injection of imported water. He could feel his shoulders relax more with each mile, and the pain of Lydia's rejection began to ease. He knew that he was spending money that he should be saving, but he also knew what he was doing was right for him.

A half hour later, Greg's GPS indicated that he was close to the address of the rental. He carefully followed the prompts up a narrow, dusty road, doing his best to avoid the large ruts on either side. When the GPS told him that he had arrived, Greg slowed to a crawl and looked to his left and right. No house. *Crap, I hope I haven't been taken.*

Not willing to give up and hear the Lydia living in his head tell him what an idiot he was, he considered his next move. He remembered passing a small convenience store a few miles back. Maybe they knew something about the house or owner.

The bell over the door announced his arrival but the man behind the counter continued to stare at his phone. Greg picked up a bag of chips, hoping a purchase would help break the screen's spell.

"Hi. I'm looking for a house up the road, but I can't seem to find it," Greg said as he slid the chips and a piece of paper with the hand-written address toward the clerk.

The man looked at the address and smirked. "Yeah, that's the Martin place. It's not visible from the road; you have to park and walk up the dirt path. Once you clear the hill, you'll see it."

Feeling much better, Greg thanked the man and paid for the chips. As Greg walked away, the clerk called out, "Look for the blue door."

Greg carefully retraced his route and once again found himself where the GPS insisted there was a house. He parked in a little dirt lot he hadn't noticed the first time and looked around until he saw the path the clerk had mentioned. He opened the trunk to retrieve his backpack and, as he slung it over his shoulder, wondered again how he had gotten to the point where most of his worldly possessions could fit in such a small bag.

The path leading up the hill was partially overgrown by shrubs and covered in loose rock and sand. When Greg reached the top, he looked for the house. Still nothing. Then, over to the right, nestled among some trees, he saw a door. No house, just a door.

Greg walked over to get a closer look. The door was set inside a frame and stood straight up with no visible signs of support. The robin's egg blue paint looked new, but the brass doorknob was tarnished and showed signs of wear. As he slowly circled the frame, he could see that it was no thicker than a typical door that might be found in a normal home. But there was nothing normal about it. At all. Feeling a little ridiculous, he cautiously knocked.

When he heard footsteps approaching from the other side, his first instinct was to run. However, before Greg could turn away, the door was opened by a small man whose bald head barely reached the middle of Greg's chest. Although the man's unnaturally small mouth held no hint of a smile, his large eyes looked friendly.

"Are you Mr. Martin?" Greg asked, trying his best to hide his uneasiness. "I'm Greg Trent. I have reservations for your Airbnb."

"Oh, yes, I have been expecting you. Come in." The little man opened the door fully to reveal black and white tile covering the floor of what appeared to be a large room. Greg quickly stepped back from the door and looked behind it. Nothing. He looked inside the room again and saw that the space was so vast no walls were visible; he could only see the checkerboard floor stretching off into the distance.

Greg hesitated to step inside and tried to stall for time as his mind struggled to find the logic of what he was seeing. "Um . . . my reservation is for three nights. What is the checkout time on Wednes-day?" he asked, even though he knew the answer.

"Oh, checkout time is 10 a.m., but you can never leave," the man replied.

As Greg drew a startled breath, Mr. Martin let out a laugh. "I'm sorry," he said. "I couldn't resist. It just cracks me up to see people's expressions when I say that. Checkout time really is 10 a.m." Then, he added, "But, really, you may not want to leave. Many have chosen to stay. Let's see how you feel on Wednesday."

As the man spoke, Greg experienced a wave of peace flowing throughout his body and he realized that his stress from the last few weeks had disappeared. He had sudden clarity that there was nothing behind him to lose and endless possibilities ahead. He hitched up his backpack and, after taking one last look over his shoulder, crossed the door's threshold and followed the odd little man toward wherever the black and white tiles led.

Bil with one L

Bil Fuhrer

My name is Bil. I spell it with one L. You might think this is not very important and it isn't. Most people don't even notice this minor mutation of a common nickname.

"Why only one L?" they ask. When I explain that the reason is dumb and the story boring, they become more curious. They seem to think this is an AKA to conceal a dark sordid past or perhaps serious psychological issues.

My personal opinion is that there are too many people in this world with wasted double letters in their names. Donna, Georganna, Joanne, Lloyd, Lynn, and don't even get me started on the name Kennette. No one ever asks them why they waste their time stroking those extra N's or L's or T's.

So why am I singled out? Why do I have to pay the price?

"What price?" you ask. How would you feel if you were always introduced as the person with only one of something that everyone expected two of? Isn't it possible you might feel deficient in some important way? Then there's the pun lover, that lowest form of humorist, who quips, "I guess you just decided to get the L out of there, huh?"

So here I am, writing to defend my name.

This is my story:

Once upon a time, there was a great leader named William Conqueror who was strong, handsome, tall, and young with fine blue eyes and a great personality. His friends called him Bill—with two L's—Conqueror. He lived in Normandy, a strange land where people ate snails on purpose. One day, a messenger arrived with a junk-mail advertising scroll inviting Bill—with two L's—and Matilda, his wife, to a free vacation in England, if they would agree to attend a ninety-minute presentation on castle timesharing. Bill said to Matilda, "Guinevere,"—because he hated the name Matilda—"I'm tired of sitting around watching reruns of the Visigoth invasions. What say I and you take a vacation over in England, drink their flat, tepid beer, and bask in the Dover fog? How does that sound?"

Matilda thought that saying "you and I" sounded better than "I and you" but otherwise agreed that a trip to England was a sterling idea.

Trouble started immediately upon their arrival. A high-pressure sales rep. named Harold, from the 11th Century, thumb screwed Bill into a contract. Issues about leaky thatch, moat mold, and Bill's attempt to pay with Visa, which Harold deemed subprime, went unresolved. Bill eventually tired of negotiating from afar and decided to invade. This was more difficult than he expected because the year was 1066 CE and the Chunnel between France and England was not yet built. They had to go by Harold's ferry, which never ran on time, and wouldn't have run at all if Harold had known what Bill was up to. Bill and his troops landed near the village of Hastings, where residents believe animal organs are edible, stuff them into pies, and eat them.

Bill wanted his troops to identify him easily, so he carried a big sign that said Bill—with two L's—and had an arrow pointing down at his helmet. When Harold saw this, he immediately created his own sign showing a picture of a huge, flattened frog and the words *Take This*. War cries echoed through the hills when the opposing forces charged.

Bowmen's arrows whistled and swords clanged as soldiers struggled in hand-to-hand combat. Death cries followed and blood flowed like a raging river through the once peaceful valley. Suddenly, an enemy soldier wielding an ax attacked Bill from behind. Bill shielded himself with his sign but the enemy's heavy weapon sliced through it, right between the two L's. The severed L fell into the scarlet stream and was swept away, forever lost. The attacker was decapitated, and Bil, now with only one L, led his troops on to victory. He sliced Harold to slivers and stomped on his frog sign. Then he stood on a mount before the conquered masses, waved his severed sign, and yelled, "We kicked butt."

Most in the crowd were illiterate, but on that historic day, they looked up at Bil and read his sign. "Bil," they cheered. It was the first word they learned on their path to literacy.

Bil—with one L—became their symbol of victory: victory for Bil Conqueror, victory for the Normans, victory for humankind, and literacy for the masses.

To this day, Bil—with one L—means all of this and serves as a reminder to others that . . . *we kick butt*.

What the L?

Keith Cervenka

I know a guy named Bil

Realy, with just one L

He won't tel me what happened to the other L

I just hope it wasn't something appaling

Was it pilaged from his mean older brother?

Was it pilfered by a colege buddy from Pen State I wonder?

He said he met his future wife at a Nittany Lion footbal game

It seemed the blue and white pom-poms were caling his name

The way she looked that night puled him into love

Like a waterfal it came from above

I wonder, did he fil her in straight away about the missing L?

I'm guessing she found out later, which is probably just as wel

So, we say farewel to the L and may the future be brighter

Because he can also be caled a darn fine writer

But, al the same, I think he'd be thriled

And his heart would be filed

If he could onlly find that missing L

An Ode to My Grandmother

Susheela Narayanan

The long lazy summer stretched before us as we fled the sweltering plains of Delhi and retreated by train to my grandmother's house in South India. She lived in the coastal town of Madras, situated on the Bay of Bengal. The days were hot and humid, but the evenings brought the welcome cooling sea breezes. The sparkling sandy shores of Marina Beach, one of the longest in the world, were a short walk away. The old house echoed with laughter and noisy chatter as many of my aunts arrived with their children, taking a welcome break from husbands and daily chores. For the womenfolk it was a constant round of chopping vegetables and nonstop cooking to feed the hungry horde multiple times a day, but it was tempered with jokes and good-humored gossip. For us children it was a carefree unfettered time as we ran up and down the stairs and played games in the spacious hall upstairs, away from prying parental eyes.

I see this slight, rounded figure wrapped in a voluminous nine-yards sari, which is what South Indian women wore in the early 1900s, sitting in a woven cane chair on the enclosed front porch of that house. It was elevated above street level so one could see the front gate and all the people passing by. Sparse yellowing grey hair pulled back tightly into a knot, wrinkled brown face, slightly unfocused eyes, and a somewhat rolling gait, wearing no jewelry except for a pair of flashing diamond earrings, probably given to her as part of her dowry. Every morning she sat there and read the newspaper painstakingly from cover to cover, with Tiger, her faithful German shepherd dog (a prized gift from her Army son) by her side. She was an ordinary figure (never given to dressing up or beautifying herself), no different from the many elderly women of her generation who lived in the neighborhood, walking to and from the temple down the road or exchanging gossip while they carefully chose the best vegetables from the street vendors, constantly haggling with them for the lowest price. But her life was by no means ordinary.

Born around 1905, Kamala, or Paati as we addressed her affectionately in Tamil, my mother tongue, was the second oldest child in a family of ten. As a teenager I heard how she was allowed to stay in

18

school only until the third grade and was soon married off when she reached puberty—as was often the case with girls at that time. I shivered to hear her describe how she gave birth to her first son at sixteen, followed in fairly quick succession by five girls and three boys.

She has described the terror of living through World War II when black papered windows were the norm, and they would dive under the tables at the sound of the sirens. As a British colony they were often under attack by the Japanese. My well-educated grandfather died young from chronic asthma, from lack of adequate medical treatment, leaving her a young widow with few skills and little education. Before he died, he made sure to teach Paati the rudiments of the English language, including how to sign her name in English—a necessary skill she needed to conduct her own financial affairs at the bank. Amazingly, this unassuming woman navigated her financial business quite successfully on her own.

My cousins and I played hide and seek in the spacious backyard, shaded by tall coconut palms waving their fronds in the sea breeze. The highlight of our vacation was waiting to harvest the green, prickly *Artocarpus Heterophyllus* (also known as jackfruit or durian in the western world) that grew on a big tree in the corner. "Paati, is it ready?" we asked excitedly every day, only to be met with a firm "not yet!"

Then finally it was the day. Paati tackled the onerous task of cutting and cleaning the heavy jackfruit, assisted by my tall, strapping younger cousin, as the rest of us watched round-eyed. She oiled her hands liberally up to her elbows with sesame oil to counteract the sticky residue from the prickly skin of the fruit, hitched her sari up to her knees and sat down on a low stool on the back veranda. Grasping the prickly fruit firmly between her feet she sliced into it with a sharp cleaver.

The intensely sweet pods were concealed in a thin papery white membrane that had to be peeled back to reveal the juicy, golden goodness inside. As we stood in an anxious circle around her, she placed a couple of pods of fruit in each outstretched hand and shooed us out to the backyard where any mess we made could be easily washed off.

Ahh . . . the indescribable taste of the first sweet bits of jackfruit hitting our tongues and dribbling down our chins! Next to a juicy golden mango this was my favorite fruit. The backyard was our hangout anytime we were given anything juicy or sweet to eat—we could be as messy as we wanted.

As teatime rolled around, Patti could be seen crouched before a small kerosene stove in the hot kitchen (in the days before gas stoves became the norm). She fried sweet crunchy "appams" in a wok of hot oil for tea as she wiped the sweat dripping from her face with the ends of her sari. Sometimes she made sweet, sticky sugar syrup to roll peanuts in for making kadalakai urundai (peanut brittle balls). She also made kai murukku, painstakingly forming the salty round braided coils of rice flour on a damp cloth before frying them in hot oil—delicious!

As a child I loved the dark intense taste of South Indian filtered coffee—but my mother disapproved of it. When coffee was served at Paati's house I would look at it longingly, not daring to ask for a sip. Paati would give me a meaningful look and give a slight nod towards the kitchen. I'd find a small cup of coffee, or whatever other treats my mom did not approve of, tucked away in the kitchen for me. She often stepped in to circumvent my mother's more severe discipline.

Paati was proud of my academic successes—something that she never got a chance to achieve. She was not an overly demonstrative or talkative woman, but I never doubted her love and support. Could she ever imagine the privileged life her grandchildren would lead on foreign shores?

Paati was a shining beacon of grit and quiet courage to our family. The deck was stacked against her in so many ways, but she plodded on with courage and independence. She is long gone now, but as her extended family thrives all over the world, she is the invisible glue holding us all together.

Do Geese See God?

Lloyd Hill

4:11 a.m. I'm eyeballing the Red Wolf Super Blood Moon
from the walkway in front of my apartment, wondering who

names celestial objects. It is about 90 percent eclipsed,
a bronze ball with a gold crescent on the upper right. I'm thrilled

in a drowsy way like Coleridge who may have thought
that geese saw God being up in the clouds so close to Heaven.

The earth is having magnetic disturbances now and who wouldn't
with sun flare-ups and 100 billion neutrinos penetrating everything

every second, even at night, at light speed through rock and flesh
whoosh, makes my fingernails hurt to think about it.

Man is not made for happiness. Man is made for fighting ferocious
beasts for food, but as long as there is death there is hope.

I can say anything I want now. "Hello Mr. Death. I take pride
that I can be friends with almost anybody. Why not you!"

4:15 a.m. I wipe my eyes and when I look the moon is clouded out
I become a re-namer of heavenly bodies: Godly glorious ghostly…

What Next?

Georganna Holmes

If you overlook a devastation or two,
say two World Wars and one Civil
(though what is civil about a war
I do not know…)

Then you must admit
we've had a fairly peaceful
historic past.
Is that not so?

We've explored, investigated,
established, extrapolated,
pushed boundaries coast to coast
as God hath wrought, instigated.

Now the question is, what next?
Saturn, Mars?
Does our future lie among
the everlasting stars?

Reflection

Frank Primiano

A pair of male deputies, and a civilian in overalls, huddled beside a deep depression in the surrounding flat farmland. Still covered with stubble from the last harvest, the field was now mud. Wisps of smoke rose from the pit. At its bottom lay a skeleton devoid of charred flesh, but partially covered by what the men decided must be the ashes of clothing.

Sheriff Bo Ronson drove the department's SUV much too fast on a road still slick from the deluge that lingered as drizzle. He squinted when the morning sun, at random intervals, broke through the clouds to shine in his eyes. Strapped in, riding shotgun, Deputy Sally Dearly braced her hands against the dash fearing a skid and collision.

"Did you hear the latest forecast?" Ronson asked. "Another tornado warning. We might not have time to finish checking out the damage from yesterday's."

"I wonder what shape the body's in," the deputy said. Without warning, the skid came, but was controlled as the sheriff pulled onto the shoulder behind a parked cruiser.

Shaking clods from their feet every few steps, Ronson and Dearly trudged through the saturated soil to the site. Their noses wrinkled and eyes teared from the odor and irritation of the smoldering remains. Among the bones, they could see slivers of unscorched wood impaled in the earth, protruding through the rib cage.

"Is this what you called in about?" Ronson asked.

"Sure is," a deputy said, "even though there ain't much left of it."

"So, what happened?"

"Mr. Furman, here, can tell you better than me."

"Hi, Melvin," the sheriff said, extending his hand.

They shook as the farmer began. "Well, me and Mama, that's the wife, was hunkered in the house, against the howlin' wind. She was just sayin' how lucky we was that the twister touched down more'n a mile away and missed us, when stuff started fallin' outa the sky. By

23

then it was moonless-night-black out. Even so, the yard light was on and we could make out what things was as they blew by. Would you believe it? A trailer, and the door of an outhouse, and a dumpster went flyin' overhead."

"What about this mess?"

"Well, next thing we seen is a shower of busted up lumber. An' sailin' along, right in the midst of all them wood scraps, was what 'peered t'be a body, arms and legs flappin', with a cape trailin' behind.

"I says, 'What was thet?' And Mama says, 'Looked like a man with a bunch of wood staves stickin' outa him like a pork-o-pine.'"

"It traveled above your house?" The sheriff jotted notes on a pad.

"Yes, sir, and fast. It tumbled down from that height all the way over here. It musta made this crater when it hit. I reached for my coat and told Mama, 'I'm gonna see what thet was.' But she grabs my arm an' says, 'No, you don't, Mister. Not in this weather, in the dark, and leavin' me here all alone.' So I says, 'But what if that be a man?' And she says, 'Ain't nothin' nobody can do fer him now.' So, we went to bed and waited till mornin' light. That's when we seen smoke from over this direction. We figured it was all that wood burnin'. I grabbed a shovel and rake, hopped on my tractor, and drove here." Mr. Furman paused for a breath.

"You put the fire out?" the sheriff asked.

"Nope. By the time I got here it was done. All what's left is right there: a bare skeleton with wood shards juttin' outa it."

"Yes, I see," the sheriff said, peering into the hole.

"Mama called you guys. And that's all I know."

Ronson finished his notes and put the pen and pad in his pocket. "Thank you, Melvin. I'm going down there now and take a closer look. Care to join me, Dearly?"

"Right behind you, Boss." The two half-stepped, half-slid, on the slippery earth to crouch beside the putrid, still-smoking, human-ap-pearing assemblage of bones.

In the SUV, after he and Sally Dearly finished scraping as much mud as they could from their boots, Bo Ronson fussed with the radio. "Hey, Dispatch, call the coroner. Tell him to get over to Furman's farm right now. I have what's left of a body he needs to collect before the next tornado blows it away." The sheriff signed off and turned to his deputy. "What do you make of that scene?"

She said, "I dunno. A body falls from the sky at night, in the rain, catches fire in the morning leaving a pristine skeleton—with no soft tissue residue. And wood stuck through it not even singed."

"Yeah, but did you notice something else strange? For having smashed into the ground, there wasn't one fracture I could see."

"You're right," Dearly said.

"And how about the skull? The teeth? Notice the upper canines?" The sheriff opened his mouth and pointed to his own. "They were long and pointy, sorta like fangs."

Mumbling, more to himself than to his deputy, Ronson continued, "If the coroner can't get DNA from those baked bones, he may have to rely on the teeth for identification."

Both retreated into silence while they mentally reviewed their observations.

The sheriff snapped his fingers. "Do you have a compact with you?" he asked Dearly.

"Of course. I may be a cop, but I'm still a lady."

"Let me borrow it. While we're waiting for the coroner, I want to go back in that hole and look at the skeleton again . . . with a mirror."

The Growler

Dave Schmidt

Using the YUM mantra to dive into the unconscious
rapidly repeating the mantra prior to falling asleep
all the while focusing intently on my heart chakra.
Felt restless, seemed a long time then sleep came.

Next found myself on a raft, floating down river
using a long white flexible pole, steers my direction.
Right behind me, a kangaroo jumps out of the water
blue colored, adult sized, glowing dark-circled eyes.

At first it looked directly at me with a menacing stare
then began to hop in my direction as if to attack
I instinctively pointed the long pole toward his chest
tried pushing him back, but he bobbed back and forth.

Now desperate, I rotated the pole toward the downstream
lodged the end and allowed the current to pole vault me
straight up and over by the riverbank, landed in a quagmire.
Useless to struggle, only found myself sinking deeper.

The creature pursued me, hopping around the quicksand
he made haunting and loud coughing growl sounds
next jumped off me, pushing my head and body down.
By now could hardly breathe, and I awoke in a panic.

The Fermi Paradox: Are We Alone?

Nan Valerio

"Hello. Is anyone out there?"

As a retiree, life can get dull and humdrum. Then, I ponder reports that I watch on the TV news or science specials. A number of programs have been about space, especially commemorating the Apollo 11 moon landing of just over half a century ago. More recently, mechanical probes have taken us exploring the surface of Mars, while the scientific community awaits the return of rock scraped from an asteroid. Meanwhile, a ring of radio telescopes listens for signals from throughout the universe.

That's when my mind awakens and I ask myself: Is anyone out there? Or, are we truly alone?

In 1950, physicist Enrico Fermi reportedly made this a topic of conversation at a lunch with other prominent scientists at the Los Alamos lab. Ever since, there have been numerous discussions of this question, now named the Fermi Paradox.

If we are alone, then there is nobody out there in space, just rocks and gas planets. So, I ask myself, why do we have to spend gobs of money to go out in space and touch them? What if we learn positively that there are no active lifeforms there? Were our tax monies wisely spent?

So far, four nations have successfully landed exploratory equipment on the moon, which we all know is just right up in the sky, easy to spot. No extraterrestrials have been found there. Now we learn that even Mars appears to be currently devoid of such beings, too.

Scientists in the International Space Station have cameras and other equipment. A number of space observatories, such as the Hubble, take pictures of stars. They might be looking at places to go and lifeforms to meet.

NASA sent plaques displaying human figures on Pioneer and golden records containing pictures and sounds of Earth on Voyager space probes. They continue to wander in space, thus demonstrating that it's hard to send a specific message if we don't have the address.

Do we really care if we are alone?

Wouldn't it be okay to be alone?

But, what if we are not alone?

Where is everybody? Or anybody?

Should we go looking? Where should we look?

How do we contact other planets, especially *Goldilocks* planets, those just-right-for-life places, in other solar systems? There are presumed to be so many of them that we have our pick. The near systems are only four or five light years away, almost "next door."

Can we get there?

I've heard about the distances and time to get there, wherever *there* might be. Will we still find anyone, even if it is doable to go to the nearest likely-inhabited neighbor? At best, the travel time and distance are, say, five years times the 5.88 trillion miles at the speed of light per year, less a few miles so we don't go backward in time, or whatever it was that Einstein said.

Yet, if some life forms are out there, why haven't they contacted us?

Why haven't they sent us a message? Are they asleep?

Are they waiting for us to make that first call?

Do they even want a call?

If they don't send us a radio message giving us their number, is that the message?

In discussion of the Fermi Paradox, scientific papers have described a dozen or more intellectually rational reasons as to why we have had no contact.

However, we don't know if these are the very same reasons that our possible cosmic-neighbors have.

Do we care?

Couldn't we be satisfied with learning more about ourselves: our own planet's many concerns, our own near-miss asteroids, and our own solar system? Don't all of us have better things to do?

Why do we need to be in contact with "our neighbors" and add to the consternation and perplexities and problems that we already have on our own little blue home?

With such a lack of evidence for any positive resolution of the Fermi Paradox, I'm running out of interest in this subject, the National Intelligence Report on Unidentified Aerial Phenomena, the U.S. Air Force, and Area 51 notwithstanding.

There must be so many more issues, without easy answers, that I could find to muse over in retirement. I'll need to start looking.

Maybe next week.

20,000 Leagues Under the Sea

Margaret Wafer

When I was eight, I snuck out of the house with my library book,
ran to the backyard and into our playhouse. Out of all seven of us,
I cherished it the most.
There was a rickety chair, a small table and a tiny window
overlooking our grassy yard.
After six months of snow, finally the scent of lilac.
And the sweet nectar we sucked out of the stems every spring.

When I wasn't playing baseball,
I sought treasure with Captain Nemo under the sea,
reading even when dusk was sinking into darkness.

I escaped my father reminding us that money doesn't grow on trees,
my brothers fighting over who would deliver the newspapers.
And me, pulling the bed covers off my sister
so we wouldn't be late for school,
Dad fuming in the car.

I boarded the Nautilus with its Captain,
swirling currents of blue rocking the playhouse.
Our backyard alive
with sea cucumbers, massive turtles,
coral reefs, and a giant squid.

Ponds of Remembrance

Maria Kotsaftis

"Verrà la morte e avrà i tuoi occhi . . ."
—Cesare Pavese
"Remembrance is a form of meeting . . ."
—Khalil Gibran

In the famous poem included in the homonymous collection by the Italian writer Cesare Pavese, this haunting line appears twice. It roughly translates as "death will come and have your eyes." Starkly put, this is *The Way of all Flesh*. Meanwhile, people enter, stay, and exit your life. Sometimes even just a fleeting previous encounter will drift back to you. You may be walking or peeling potatoes or even better—ironing—and for no apparent reason, there the person is again. Somebody you have forgotten you remembered will come floating back to you, and it eerily feels as if they are standing there beside you once again.

In Greek Orthodox masses "for the defunct," the phrase "May their memory be eternal" is repeated over and over. The sentiment behind that is lovely and consoling to the bereaved, but it is fleeting at best. For most of us, being commemorated boils down to our "15 minutes of fame" at a service held by loved ones in our honor. Due to circumstances, not even that is a given, as we witnessed during this pandemic around the globe.

Picture that we are sitting by a deep pond where a bright and majestic Koi decides to leave the depths, and break surface so we can admire its distinctive beauty before it returns to the impenetrable shadows. The first one to appear is of grey hue with black speckles and very few scattered orange scales. He is big, battered-looking and a far cry from the symmetric beauty ideal of the prized Koi. His tail forms anything but a perfect fan. Unkindly, he could be called hideous by comparison to a prime specimen, as he is disfigured with lots of scales missing and scars galore.

This is a man I used to see coming up the stairs from the underground station where I grew up in Munich. I was a teenager returning in the afternoon from a long day at school, and he was descending the stairs in the opposite direction. The first time I laid eyes on him I was initially startled and then shocked, and even though I caught myself and tried not to let on, I am sure he realized anyway. He must have been in an accident, and facial surgery was a long way from becoming all the rage it is now, let alone affordable, so what I saw was not instantly recognizable as a human face. The famed "Elephant Man" comes to mind, and at first my brain was not able to compute. The facial deformity was exacerbated by burned patches that marred his skin. His battered face was framed by a mane of long, straight, light-brown hair.

He must have been young. From the neck down nothing was out of the ordinary: a tall, skinny but sportive body in tight leather pants and an exceedingly cool, long, flowing, distressed brown leather coat. Barring the face, he could have been on the cover of a rock 'n roll magazine. Was he in a motorcycle accident? Did something literally blow up in his face? I saw him several times, always in the same spot on the stairs to the underground and always with the flowing leather coat that fanned out like a veil as he swiftly made his way down. I recall us acknowledging each other nonverbally with a mutual nod, once I had transcended my initial fear and was able to look at him despite of what I saw. What courage it must have taken to go through life like that and to notice people's reactions each day. He must have lived close by.

After years, having moved away and coming back to visit old neighbors, whom do I see in the exact same spot as always, as if we had a tacit rendezvous of eternally crossing paths? Me going up and him coming down the stairs to the underground, both of us a lot older. I noticed a slight startled motion in an otherwise frozen face followed by the usual nod, indicating he must have recognized me too, despite all the time that had passed. This was "our moment" and I have not seen him since. Yesterday as I was taking a walk in our neighborhood, an ocean and a continent away from where I started, he drifted right back up to me from the bottom of oblivion. After observing him for a while, I shall let this battered Koi submerge itself back into the depths of the pond with my blessings and gratitude.

◇◇◇

The leaves are rustling above, a light breeze plays on our faces and the sun sends an occasional ray through to shine on the water's surface stirring the curiosity of another Koi swimming towards the light. This one is smaller, a pure white color with a big round red spot right on its forehead. His name is Bryan. He told me after years of passing him twice a day under the bridge where he lived.

Of slight build, with dirty blond hair and John Lennon glasses that gave him an almost scholarly look, I could not help but notice him on my daily trips taking my sixth-grade son Nikita to and from school. In the morning he was usually still asleep lying motionless in his sleeping bag next to an old shopping cart containing his few belongings. Later in the afternoon he would sometimes be talking to himself or carefully inspecting his navel. At other times he would just let the world go by, looking at the steady stream of cars exiting or ascending the freeway ramp. He seemed to be in his late thirties, and I forget how exactly our first encounter played out, but somehow it did.

From then on, I made it a point to make him an occasional sandwich or let him partake of some of my homecooked meals, and sometimes Nikita and I took him a burrito from the nearby Mexican takeout place. He loved those. On cold, rainy mornings, when thinking about him sleeping out under the damp bridge just about killed me, I would leave some hot tea or a coffee next to where he was sleeping, so he would find it upon awakening. Sometimes when we were late driving to school, I would have Nikita get out of the car while I waited inside. At first, my son was wary and a bit afraid of startling the sleeping man who had once yelled at him on a bad day. I can still see Nikita carefully walking the distance looking back at me for reassurance and gingerly depositing whatever we had that day.

Once we got to know each other better, though, Bryan would wave at us and walk up to the car, if I stopped. I slipped him a nail clipper once after I had seen his hands that looked like talons, but I don't think he ever used it. Every now and then I admit I gave him a pack of *Muratti* cigarettes from my secret stash, because Bryan was a heavy smoker. His encampment was so densely littered with cigarette butts that they almost formed a brown carpet on the dirt floor.

At another time, when the city was holding a special event for the homeless, I passed info to Bryan. People could get free haircuts, medical checkups, some supplies and find out about resources in general. He ended up not going but he told me that he was on a waiting list for veterans to move into more permanent housing. This alerted me that his occasional rants must have been a souvenir from the second US war with Iraq and probably PTSD-induced.

Then Nikita was suddenly done with Middle School and the new school was elsewhere. I went back to look for Bryan but his usual spot lay abandoned. He had told me on numerous occasions that police had ordered him to leave. Usually, he would come back though. On the side of the bridge there was a lush green hillside with trees surrounded by a chain-link fence from whence he sometimes emerged. A friend who still had a child at the school told me Bryan was no longer there. That year there was a terrible Hepatitis B outbreak that ripped through San Diego's homeless population and claimed many lives. The city put up a tent encampment to temporarily house people and to contain the spread during the outbreak. I want to believe that Bryan was taken there and that a spot on the housing waitlist opened up for him. I wish for him to have found a home, so he could live safely and with dignity—as he deserves.

◇◇◇

The light by the pond has changed and the shadows are growing longer. A slight chill has crept into the crepuscular air; you should zip up your jacket. It is about time to leave. But look at this splendid specimen of a Koi that has appeared on the surface for a last round before tucking in for the night. He is a real stunner: bright orange, big, and with a spectacular tail wafting in elegant splendor. His name is Ron.

Rugged good looks in the vein of Gary Cooper, he was tall with beautiful wavy hair always perfectly styled in a cut reminiscent of the leading men of Hollywood's golden era. I would see him in the neighborhood, usually smoking a cigarette. In fact, I first consciously noticed him when for a while he had stationed himself opposite our house on a little wall that winds around the schoolyard across the street. He would just sit there looking across, smoking his cigarette and watching things unfold. We had a toddler then and another baby on the way, so we were in and out a lot. At first, I was startled and a bit un-nerved by his prolonged daily presence and persistent "loitering" as the English language calls it. He never said anything, just sat there smok-ing, but we had acknowledged each other's presences somehow. I asked a neighbor who was walking his dog whether he knew anything about the man. He didn't, but to my great regret he walked right up to him and said something. That is when his contemplative taciturn sessions across from us came to an end.

I was teaching Italian at the time and one of my adult students said she grew up on our street. When I asked her which house, it turned out to be the big double-story one, four houses down from us. She also said that it had since been converted to a home where a community of men was living under the supervision of a lady with a young boy and various other staff. In the big backyard, there was a jungle gym and a set of swings and tables and chairs, but I rarely saw anyone sitting out there. That is when it dawned on me that my "loiterer" must be one of the people living there. I started to notice medical vans pulling up and people coming and going. Over the years his hair turned salt-and-pepper which made him look distinguished, and had he worn a suit instead of jeans and a dark blue baseball jacket, he could have been taken for a charismatic politician.

When our kids were in elementary school, we would leave the house at the same time each morning and pass a group of the inhabitants waiting outside, and although "Mr. Handsome" could not maintain extended eye contact, he would always wave and flash us a brief smile. Seeing him en route to school had become our beautiful morning ritual. When our daughter started high school, we had to leave the house much earlier, so that is when we stopped encountering our local "Marlboro Man" on a regular basis. On very few occasions afterwards I caught a glimpse of him walking with a cigarette between his lips, but he was more distant now, being elsewhere with his thoughts or perhaps heavily medicated. A few weeks ago, it occurred to me that I had not seen him in a very long while. On one of my "sanity walks" during lockdown, as I passed the house, the nurse was coming out ready to walk around the block with the men for their daily exercise. I decided to ask about Mr. Handsome and described him. She laconically said that he had passed on a couple of years previously. I wanted to be able to refer to him, so I asked what his name was. His name was Ron.

◇◇◇

The Koi are sleeping now at the bottom of the pond, no ripples on the surface and the moon mirrors itself in the calm waters.

Cosmic Romance

Mary Thorne Kelley

4 "Romance"
from the *Masquerade Suite* of
Aram Khachaturian

Once, two planets alike in essence
from their orbits strayed away
and wandered, lone and restless,
until they chanced to meet near here one day.

A collision did much damage
to their independency—
they fused soon as though to banish
forevermore all separate entity.

But, before the fire could cool,
all their substance to compound,
a bolt struck! Out from a black cloud
and their union endeavored to confound.

Even so, it was not destined
that black Fate should thus prevail.
Hence their union evolved a New State,
everlasting each succeeding Life!

Here but Gone

Katherine Porter

We each cross our right leg over our left. My hands remain safely stowed under my thighs until I sweep hair from my eyes. His hair has receded to nothing, so he rakes fingers through a beard—the closest thing he can do to mirror my move.

Are we in sync? Maybe.

Rocking on the porch swing, we sway like parakeets. Our silence is stunning, save for the gentle *swoosh* of our perch. The sun streams through the bougainvillea to bake my knees exposed below my shorts. Testing for sunburn, my finger pushes on the skin—blood disperses. Releasing the pressure—blood rushes back. My knees smolder, just like my anger.

Is this man really my father? Maybe.

A dragonfly appears and alights on my burnt knee. I know it is a she because I maintain a love affair with insects, which began in high school and persists. Back then, life was simple: catch a bug, identify it, place it in a killing jar with a cotton ball soaked with fingernail polish remover, stick a pin through its thorax, and mount it in a wooden bug coffin. Now, life is complicated: husband, kids, house, bills, and all their never-ending complexities. Why, then, has this creature, in a simple act, chosen my warm skin as the spot for an afternoon rest? Doesn't she have an instinct for danger? I may kill her for my collection.

Perhaps nature is alerting me to the synchronicity of earth, sky, wind, and love.

I look at the man beside me and at the bags under his eyes, his balding head, his fat fingers. He isn't the perfect father specimen I'd imagined, but I have found him, and he is the only one I'll have. I imagine the huge bottle of ethyl acetate and the giant pin necessary to keep this being in place.

The dragonfly tickles my skin. As a teenager, I composed poetry in my head. That was twenty years ago. But writing poetry is like riding a bicycle: when learning how, it keeps dumping you on the pavement, and you can't help getting back up for more.

Poetic phrases pop like firefly flashes in my brain.

> A red-bodied helicopter
> with silver wings as see-through
> as lace tat-tat tatted
> she lugs a massive twitching head
> windshield eyes, wrap-around windows
> reflecting all colors, seeing all things
> a rainbow world
> Oops,   gone in a flash

She takes off, and my mind is back to hunting for something to say to this man, my father. He glances at me, and a slight smile appears on his lips. Again, she lands on the exact spot as though it is home. Poetry returns.

> Returning to this warm surface
> a sunny knee blushed with pink
> she wears a brick-colored hairy wrap
> her thin tail tattooed with black
> she stands still but pumps
> up . . . and down, up . . . and down

My father is breathing in the same rhythm—in . . . and out, in . . . and out. Should I call him "Dad" even though it doesn't feel right? Am I ready to forgive that he abandoned Mom to raise me alone? A second dragonfly arrives.

> A male darts into view
> his colors flashing green
> he flies backward, does a 180
> returns and docks upon the knee
> Will he stay? A moment later
> Oops,   he's gone in a flash

> She's alone
> her legs as dainty as black twigs with feet
> four down and two up, she paws the air

reaches to smell a fly, a mosquito, a gnat
multitudes to eat today, her jaws will gnash
Oops,   she's gone in a flash

Back again
he hovers with silent flying perfection
at thirty beats per second
he flutters above this planet, above this knee
will he make contact?
Oops,   gone in a flash

"Are you okay?" my father asks attempting to make contact.

I notice his cigarette breath, too close, and wipe a tear from my cheek. "Just watching those dragonflies," I say. "Did you see them?"

"No," he answers and scans the air by swiveling side to side. His searching intensifies. "My wife says I never notice anything." He sighs. He gives up.

Tears speed down my cheeks. I need him to be someone who will notice me, who will never give up again, even though his wife is not my mom, even though he and I don't know each other. Realizing I have no patience for a man who isn't aware of more than his own thoughts, I release a sigh of my own. I give up. "I don't think I'm ready to have you in my life."

He shakes his head. "I was afraid of that. Do you want me to go?"

There's been no apology. Calling him "Dad" feels risky, but I decide to try it once. "Look, Dad, I'm thirty-eight, and you never looked for me. I don't know where we go from here."

"I'm not going anywhere," he says and reaches for my hand.

As though shooing away a flying pest, I brush his hand away. Then I stand up, run down the porch, and leap off the steps.

"Gone in a flash," he calls out.

I stop. We are in sync. The earth spins below, clouds drift across the sun, and a fierce wind arrives at my back to shove me forward— away from him. But I don't move. I can't move. Do I want to? My feet feel planted in indecision. Risk, a burden bolstered by the past, weighs on my shoulders, on my heart. I turn to face him. He's standing on the porch edge. I will not go to him even though his arms reach toward me. Will he cross this distance between us? He won't.

"Not yet," I say, swivel, sprint away, and almost take off in flight.

Celestial Combatants

Susie Parker

Dawn steals the sky from the Night,
sneaks in under a veil of mist
so gently,
Night doesn't even notice.
Dawn claims more and more
of their shared territory,
until Night is vanquished.
Night gathers strength,
across the globe,
swarms back, armed with stars.

Serendipity

Linda Smith

Sometimes you get lucky enough
to outlive your demons,
the past

what trapped before
now shed, you
emerge
butterfly
closed eyes
shoulders relaxed
body bends
sways side-to-side
feet touch hard wood floor
explore
what supports you
explore

again
pick up where you left off
pick up what you laid down
begin again thankful
for new vision, thankful
for *this* moment
this light

Grace Comes in Waves

Lindsay Elise Reph

Sunday afternoon, the next scene of our own little movie is upon us, ready or not. Mom assures me that my makeup looks "so pretty, Sweetie," and helps me apply mascara. Certain I'll jab the goopy wand into my eye and create a new injury, I request she finish the ragtag makeover for me. Just like I practiced, I fold the silk scarf in half diagonally and tie it around my head, neatly tucking stray hairs away where nobody will have to look at them.

I choose the black pants with the tie in front and a black V-neck T-shirt because they seem most appropriate under the mock-denim-print spinal stabilization vest that I must wear whenever seated upright. Not that anything about me is appropriate for the real world, where capable, attractive people roam freely. I'm only being released into the wild for a practice lap, mangled and dragging my hind legs.

The thought of sitting in a wheelchair at a restaurant in the bustling Bay Area, interacting with random strangers, and somehow keeping my food down makes me painfully anxious. It turns my stomach to picture an awkward toilet transfer in the ladies' room. The way I have to touch the seat and grab the handles for dear life will be much more disgusting in a public restroom. After quietly attempting to dehydrate all day, I use the toilet once in the hospital bathroom before we leave and pray that I won't have to go again until we return.

By the time I'm seated shotgun in Mom's BMW, waiting for her to fold up the wheelchair and load it into the trunk, I'm already exhausted. If she hadn't been working so hard to execute this important outing, I'd beg to go back to bed. This could still count as PT.

"Okay," Mom says as she gets in, closes the door, and puts her hands on the steering wheel. "Where to?"

"Let's just go to Marie Callender's," I answer, having gone through the options at length yesterday. I feel like Henry Fonda in *On Golden Pond*, cranky and wary of going out in public. I don't want to go anywhere there's a crowd. I don't want the ambience or other patrons to be too loud, too friendly, or too trendy. I want to blend in if that's at all possible and—though I know it isn't—I'm trying to hide behind a few safe delusions. I want food that is bland, American, and least likely to come back up in the midst of a busy restaurant. I want to return confident that, after nearly three months, I'm finally ready to be discharged from hospitals for good.

"Chicken Pot Pie, please." I order a comfort food from childhood when the server comes. I can barely tolerate small talk because it's not the real me we're talking about. I make my best neutral face as Mom shares tidbits to quench questions and curious looks, "Serious car accident . . . multiple surgeries . . . ninety days in hospitals . . . lucky to be alive . . ."

That's not me.

The real me lives by the beach in San Diego, rides a skateboard, works in a café, earned a bachelor's degree in psychology, and has a group of friends called "The Fam" who are waiting for me to get home in time for Happy Hour at "The Shine."

That's me.

If I can't be me anymore, I need to learn to be somebody else. Somebody I can know. As conversations swirl around the restaurant, reality bears down on me, making my brain throb. I nibble at the pot-pie and push food around my plate like a child with poor table manners. My appetite has fled along with my long hair and pretty face, never to be seen again. I feel so out of place that I yearn to be back inside hospital walls, where I'm safe and unnoticeable, where I really belong. I decide to call it quits after using only half of our three-hour pass and simply say, "I'm ready to go now."

In the parking lot, Mom points out how pretty the sunset is going to be. "Look, over there; it's going to turn pink, I bet. Beautiful!" She looks from me to the orangey-pink sky and inhales a deep breath, exhaling slowly.

I wish I cared enough to appreciate it, but the sunset isn't over the beach. And I'm a shell of my former self; I don't see what's so beautiful about it. I feel like a gargoyle perched in my wheelchair for everyone to gawk at, even though the parking lot is near-empty.

"Pardon me, ladies. Would you like some help?"

A woman about Mom's height, maybe a decade older, with dark hair and a wide, easy smile strides up to us seemingly out of nowhere.

"Oh, hello. That's so kind of you," Mom says.

Embarrassed to have been noticed, I wait for Mom to decline her help so we can slink away in the fading daylight. But then she continues, telling the woman why we're here, what happened, and what's ahead.

I try to melt into the wheelchair.

After patiently hearing Mom out, the lady says, "I can help load the chair; I've done it a million times." She pauses. "My daughter has spina bifida."

Mom gasps and touches the woman's arm. I wait for a sob story that doesn't come as the stranger continues, explaining that wheelchairs are tough to maneuver at first, but assuring us we've almost got the hang of it. She says her daughter is nineteen and was diagnosed at birth.

My mind begins to swirl with all of the experiences I was blessed with in the twenty-three years prior to the accident. What if I hadn't had any of them? Physical health has been a natural part of almost all of the stand-out moments in my life.

"You'll get so much better once you get home, honey. I know that as sure as I know how going out to dinner is good for the spirit, even when the body can't keep up," she says.

Mom thanks her profusely as she helps get me settled in the front seat. Together, they fold my wheelchair and load it into the trunk. In the side mirror, I see the two mothers with broken babies embrace one another.

Mom gets into the car and dabs her eyes with a tissue, starts the engine, and rolls down the windows. I feel her look at me, but she remains silent, preserving the moment. As she pulls out of the parking spot, I feel a breeze on my face and take a deep breath, drawing in the cool evening air. Maybe there is hope—at least in simple joys—and comfort in the many memories my battered brain has miraculously preserved. In the pastel Monet-sunset light, I watch the woman as she smiles, gives me a little wave, turns, and walks away.

The excerpt above from *Grace Comes in Waves* is a true story about an automobile accident that nearly claimed the lives of the author and her sister. Both survived, and after a two-week coma, multiple surgeries, and three hospitals, our protagonist is preparing to be discharged to her family home to continue rehabilitation. It has been nearly twelve weeks since the accident.

Mirror, Mirror

Dave Schmidt

The reliable mirror was always available for views
With any object nearby in its domain of coverage
Never to reveal to any other, one's private images
And when walking away, our images are gone

Countless times have I gazed into a clean mirror
And trusting a faithful replication of myself
Over time to view stages of my growth process
Or to improve on any unwanted facial features

I revere the mirror for its honesty and loyalty
And a reminder that my distress affects it not
Like my awareness is not disturbed in viewing
The tragedies and suffering in the world around me

Absorbed in a lifetime of countless experiences
In the mirror of my awareness and never forget
The necessity of cleansing with deep restfulness
To maintain a proper inner reflective mirror

Free Range

Nancy Foley

Snuggled in soft shavings under a heat lamp
are Noel, Winter & Aspen, temporary house guests.
These petite chicks peck & peep in a protected
plastic tub complete with cedar-scented sawdust
& a fresh fountain of water placed next
to a silver saucer of first-rate feed.
Holding Aspen in the cup of my hands
I gently pet her powder-puff fluff.

At six weeks, the heat lamp is removed.
They remain in the warmth of our home until
eight weeks when the chicks can handle outdoor
chills. Then they move to our daughter's home
& join hens Scrooge, Snowflake, Eve, & Ginger
in a secure fenced-in covered coop which protects
against predators that prowl the neighborhood.

At five months they start laying eggs, & grandkids Zach
& Mackenzie gather the bronze eggs from the coop
after opening the gate for these free-range chickens to roam.
Since the pandemic has kept the kids at home, they love
to chase and cuddle them. Mackenzie even pushes
gentle Ginger in her doll stroller. At feeding time
the chicks step up to the back door peeping for attention
like spoiled children. At dusk they strut back
to the coop as if returning from a day at the park.

As a volunteer at Fr. Joe's Villages in San Diego,
I notice the reoccurring *human* scene. Scrunched
in a corner on a cold-stone sidewalk sits a mother
& her three children shivering as a shadow
crosses their path. A baby stroller holds
their belongings and hands are hidden
in the pockets of threadbare coats with no
trace of silver linings. They wait patiently
in line to secure shelter for the night.
Although they are free to roam, their future
seems to say *Dead End.*

What can we do to give them wings to fly away
from homelessness, to help them find a home
as cozy and secure as a family of coddled chickens?

Like Beef Jerky

Laura Fitch

There was a body in the old Volvo. In the front passenger seat, a shiny-bald man, his brownish skin tough, dry like beef jerky, was definitely dead. She ran to the house and called the police, then went around, locking all windows and doors. She'd walked past that car many times; had she missed the body? It wasn't easy to get up here. The Volvo, covered in silvery dust, had been sitting on the road when she arrived a few days before.

The house was just like the one she grew up in, except that it was perched on a hill. A dusty road led to the front door. When she looked out the window, the car was gone. Puzzled, she wondered what else was gone. The road was gone. It was covered by what appeared to be water. Looking out toward the ocean, she saw it was rising, slowly rising, to meet her. The garden below the window was also covered with water now, and under the door, water tendrils seeped in. After running to the bedroom, and looking for—but not finding—her iPhone, she rushed to the living room, the whole time telling herself to think. Think.

She didn't want to risk going outside and being swept away or electrocuted. Water sloshed now. Hopping on top of the kitchen table, she tried to think. She should have shut off the gas. There were fires during the Japan tsunami. People survived by going to higher ground. She already was at higher ground. Was this a tsunami? Climbing onto a countertop, she was disappointed with her simple mind that could not think of a way out. Could she MacGyver it? Open a window, crawl onto the roof, make a floating device out of roof shingles?

With the water at waist level, she crawled onto the top of the refrigerator. Papers with her stories, her drawings—debris now—floated in the water unaware of their fate. It was getting dark. The water, rising still, inched closer and closer. Reaching down, she dipped her fingers, feeling the harshness of the cold ocean. She wanted to sleep. That would risk drowning, but what else could she do? She repeated loudly, "Think," so many times it turned into a prayer, a mantra, the word like in a neon sign on a billboard, or in a book with the title an

48

admonishment to think, think, the pages repeating, think, think, think, single spaced, not capitalized.

She was uncomfortable. There was barely enough room for her on the refrigerator. Creaks, thuds, and the water's incessant sloshing lulling her to sleep. Her heart, beating so fast before, settled into a slower pace. How would people identify her? She could look for a Sharpie but they were under water. Or, she could reach for a knife, carve her name into her arm, but she'd bleed. And, it would hurt, ha, ha. If they found her, they could test a DNA sample. She'd recently gotten her results back, claiming she was mostly Spanish and Native American, with low percentages of African, Filipino, and Ashkenazi Jew. The ocean didn't care.

The canoe felt fragile, made of twigs, beef jerky, bark, and leaves. It floated slowly on the current, the smell of the ocean reminding her of trips to the beach as a child. The moon, as always, illuminated the way.

Lasting Impressions of Mother

Frank Primiano

Her firstborn was a charming, precocious boy. From the very beginning, the young woman and her husband knew the child was special. As soon as he learned to talk, he surprised everyone with his profound statements. One day, as his mother cuddled him on her lap, she asked, "Who do you like better to hold you, Daddy or me?"

"You, Mommy," he replied without hesitation.

"Why?" his flattered mother asked, eager for a further compliment.

"Because you have softer pillows," he said, snuggling into her well-defined cleavage.

As one sage relative who heard the story observed: "That preference will strengthen with age."

Almost twenty years later, we are besieged by persistent entreaties from a TV huckster who wants us to buy *his* pillow. Unfortunately for him, his pleas fall on unsympathetic ears: not only those of jaded oldsters who see through the hype, but also those of that precocious boy, now a young man, who continues to recall the standard against which he will forever judge the softness of pillows—his mother's.

A Parent Is a Child's First Teacher

Katherine Porter

I pick up the biggest knife in the kitchen, walk up behind him, and bring it down with all the strength my tetherball-playing muscles can call up.

If he hadn't asked me again that day, I might not have. It's just that he'd used the knife and made stew, which I refused to eat, so that heavy blade still sat on the counter with blood on it waiting for me to wash it. It was one of my many chores, me being his braid-wearing only child.

I hated when he asked me to sit on his lap as though I owed him love. I didn't. I was sure of it because he'd already taken so much away; there wasn't much left of me. Where did he hide all the sparkle and sunshine I had when I was five? Were they stowed in the attic with other decaying treasure? When he wasn't home, I snuck up those dark, creaky stairs and peeked into every cobwebby corner and every dusty trunk. The pain I felt at not being able to find even one My Little Pony was almost too much to bear.

What I did find was a shelf with a stack of pictures, pictures of me. There I am: Jane, Jane of Pleasant Street. And pictures of us together. None of Mom. I stared at them and wondered why I couldn't recall being in any of those places or in any of those poses, smiling in that weird way that didn't show any feelings. What is this girl thinking? I asked, before placing them back where they lived among the dust bunnies. Is she really me? The girl who loves rabbits and even had a lop-eared long-haired bunny named Chester for a short while, until Dad decided he'd make that stew.

One day after he got home from work—he was a middle school PE teacher—I showed him a mysterious, colorful drawing that I'd always loved and viewed as somewhat abstract. What do you see, Dad? I wanted him to divulge some secret from his mind, perhaps from his past, as though the drawing were a test of his morals. I don't know, he said. Come sit on my lap and I'll think about it, he said. You love your dad, don't you, he said. He didn't use any questions, but I knew the answers to what he really meant to ask. I'm too old to sit on your lap.

You might be my dad, but I don't think your love is the sort any daughter wants.

But I said neither of these. Instead, I ran to my room and hid in my closet behind the red velveteen bathrobe, the one Mom sewed for me, the one where she put elastic through the wrist casings to keep out drafts, the one she wrapped for my birthday with paper covered in rainbows. She left before my special day arrived. I wear the robe and think she's hugging me.

She didn't know Dad was more than unfaithful to her. No one knew what I knew, mainly because I hardly realized it myself—baths with him and unwanted touches and fleeting images of seeing too much and him taking pictures and him using the butcher knife. Now I am twelve and I do know. I know everything. At school, a teacher talked about "private" things and why we could say "no" and tell her if we needed help.

"Ms. Jansen, I need help," I say, placing the knife on her desk.

It Takes Courage

Jean E. Taddonio

Her brain, dappled with shadows
is like summertime sun sifting through leaves
or stained glass reflections
on a chapel wall

Once striving to help others
she now strains for words, a sliver of light,
in a thousand-piece puzzle
too complex to construct

There are flickers of memory.
The grass was once green, how long ago?
And what of her beloved dog?
A husband? Yes. Once.

She is easily led to the present
by those who love her
and are willing to be humbled
by the brevity of time's passage.

Moments worthy of attention
will soon be forgotten.
It takes courage to let go
of what cannot be changed.

Jeane's Poetry

Georganna Holmes

Written for Jean E. Taddonio
and for all the poets and friends of mine
in the workshop   —Georganna Holmes

I'm in another world,
that of Jeane's poetry,
my own drear atmosphere
suspended temporarily.

Hers of imagination,
the storyteller's art,
arabesques of love,
tales of the heart.

Sorrow, sadness, tears,
then the healing
airily expressed
with tenderness of feeling.

I come back to earth
…eventually.
No, there's nothing quite like
the magic of poetry.

Once upon a Reunion

Nancy Foley

A bite of chicken drumstick, and I'm back at Liberty Park in rural Batesville, Indiana, attending our annual Laudick family reunion. Inside the picnic shelter are twelve long tables with benches, each covered with a checkered or floral vinyl tablecloth upon which sits a woven basket stuffed to the top with comfort foods: creamy potato salad, fresh-picked corn on the cob, brown sugar baked beans, juicy peach or sweet cherry pie, and not-to-be-missed batter-dipped Crisco-cooked crunchy fried chicken.

While the women exchange culinary secrets and family gossip, the men talk baseball and listen to the Cincinnati Reds game blasting from the transistor radio. Kids, including myself, my sister Gretchen and brother Michael, race to the playground to climb the monkey bars, play tag or hide and go seek, and fight over the five high-flying swings.

A long line forms at the giant slide. From the top step I can see all the way to the water tower in the distance. I wonder what the view might be if I slipped away from the park, jumped the security fence, and climbed up the ladder attached to the tower. Could I see the train station from there? What if the train was traveling to Cincinnati and I had a ticket to the Reds game? Would anyone miss me if I disappeared? "Hurry up, what are you waiting for?" I turn my head, see the trail of kids lined up like marching ants, and slide back down to earth.

At noon, Uncle George rings the tarnished brass bell that hangs in the shelter, and ninety relatives follow the aroma to the tables topped with one signature dish that each family shares: Aunt Dotty's pickled bean salad, Cousin Pauline's paprika-sprinkled deviled eggs, or Grandma's pineapple lime Jell-O. After eating my fill of drumsticks, I smile and ask Aunt Ann for one of her coconut chocolate chip cookies, saving room for the homemade vanilla ice cream in the huge metal buckets, which will be served later in the day.

Outside the picnic shelter are two enormous ice-filled galvanized steel tubs: one contains bottles of Pabst Blue Ribbon Beer for the adults; the other has bottles of orange, cherry, and grape soda pop for the kids. Near the end of the day when the ice has melted, my fingers freeze as I reach in the icy water to grab whatever is left over. At no other time in the year, if my parents are watching, am I allowed to drink not just one, but two, or even three bottles of pop.

Hearing a bee buzzing takes me back to the reunion when I am nine years old, and a swarm of bees attacks and stings my arms and legs. Uncle Paul, a Korean War veteran, rushes me to the creek and smears my body with slimy mud as tears run down my cheeks. Startled stares from the kids are more painful than the actual stings. I wonder what would happen if all of them got stung and were screaming their heads off. They'd have to wait until Uncle Paul had cared for me before he'd help them. By that time, those kids would have jumped into the creek and been soaked from head to toe with no change of clothes for the rest of the day. I straighten my shoulders and wipe away the tears.

Later in the day at each reunion, the fishermen in our family try their luck at catching Blue Gill in the slow-flowing creek; others play softball on the park's practice field; and the older folks head to the tables for Bingo. The afternoon lingers like a long-lasting lollipop. After the family history is read, photos taken, and the sun begins to set, we hug our cousins, aunts, and uncles, and pile into our Ford Country Squire station wagon for the two-hour ride. When Dad pulls into the garage at our Indianapolis home, I am asleep, dreaming of the giant slide, soda pop, and the crunchy taste of mom's "finger-lickin'" fried chicken.

This year the pandemic has restricted our extended family reunions. Gatherings are limited to ten to twenty persons, and instead of hugs, we elbow bump or bow. Sharing picnic food is strictly prohibited, and masks are advised at all times. Children are not allowed to wander, and playground equipment is chained up like caged elephants in a once-upon-a-time circus train. During the much-appreciated events when our family does gather for a barbecue, the time races by, gulped down like a shot of tequila, while I long for those lazy lollipop days.

The Road House

Tim Calaway

Asked myself why I was a hundred miles down the road
before I thought about what was once where that gas station stood.
Connections thinly made, mine to that place were gossamer.
Deleterious, perhaps, is the legacy of the Road House,
early on it might have been a thriving business in town.
From what I knew it had declined when the bypass came,
green clapboard with once white trim might have welcomed
holiday travelers on a trip from the city, or from the farmland.
It was only a short time, once off the main road, that it became the
jaundiced bar I remember, it had that Bonnie and Clyde look
kicked around by fate and the wonders of progress.
Like other small shops in town, it faded into the background,
most of the customers were locals who'd grown up with the place.
Neon signs blinked their brightness trying to reach the highway,
only to find that no one on the road could find time to stop.
Perhaps they'd had their fill at a more modern establishment.
Quaint no longer met their needs, it was another era passing away.
Road House became that den of iniquity you'd sworn to avoid.
Stark tales told to those who'd listen, stabbings so they said,
too many fights, too many cops, flashing lights replace the neon.
Understanding was never a highlight of the place, simply that local
venue for cast-offs and early drinkers who had nowhere else to go.
When did they take it down? Don't remember, it's been a while.
You could look it up, why bother. There are only townhouses now.
Zoning restrictions won't allow for any Road Houses.

Mostly Not

Bjorn Endresen

His body
well maintained
no parts worn out
fit, ready and able

His brain
full of knowledge
to share

until the neurons
slowly
wore out or
stopped firing or
died, how can I know

He knew
less
and less
and less
and the time came
when he just looked
at us, or not at us
until he stopped
looking and just *was*
or maybe he wasn't

I don't know
what he was, or *if*—
if he was happy
if happy existed
in between those
dead neurons
if he was sad

or confused
or afraid
or in pain
or nothing at all

I wished it would kill
faster
which I sometimes regret
but mostly not

Sand in Her Shoes

Sarah Powers

Dry. Scratchy. And, sticking to her bare feet, the sand she must get off quickly. Maggie had taken too much time sitting on a rock with her feet in the sand watching the waves at the La Jolla State Beach. It was her thinking place where she could sit on the seawall with her crumbly scone from the Brick & Bell and a Diet Coke, her feet dangling in the sand, watching the novice surfers attempt to get on their boards. She also loved to watch the water flowing back and forth like, well, like waves, meditating on the colors from the darkest blue velvet to the soft blue of a clear sky to the white of the foam like the top of the beer she was late for.

Maggie had trudged along, her bare feet burning on the hot sand then on the hotter pavement by her car, her joints aching with tiredness, making her wonder if, though she was only 50, she was getting too old for trips like this.

She had forgotten a towel, again, and searched the trunk of her car for anything dry-off-able, throwing around paper towels and a pile of shopping bags, all from Trader Joe's for some reason, dog toys, and bags of mismatched clothing, now a size too small, to drop off at Goodwill. After a bit more shuffling of the odds and ends stashed in her trunk, Maggie realized that the paper towels would work. "Argh," she thought as she dug them out from under the backseat where they had rolled.

"I'm so late," Maggie admonished herself as her phone rang. It was her sister. "I'm here at the pub. Where are you?" Anna asked, her voice bouncing through the words as if wanting to sing. "I'm trying to get sand off my feet," Maggie replied, her voice a pout as if this were the 10th time Anna had asked. She was meeting up with her twin and her twin's fiancé, Mike, today. Anna's younger, ballroom-dancing fiancé. Yet, he made her sister happier than Maggie had thought possible. Then, after lunch, the two were going to show her their new condo. It might only be 600 square feet, but Anna said they could see the ocean from their bedroom if they craned their necks just right.

Maggie couldn't imagine living her sister's life. Maggie's life was a parade of medical appointments and living with their mother—of limbs that tremor instead of dancing and "it's time to take your laundry out of the washer" instead of the sweet nothings of newlyweds.

"I need a couple more minutes and I'm on my way," she told Anna.

"That's OK. I was worried you weren't feeling well again today and we'd really miss seeing you.

"Nope. I'm really on my way. See you in just a few." Maggie knew that she had said that sentence hundreds of times to her sister. And her mom. And her friends. It's a constant refrain when you have a chronic illness. With fibromyalgia you never know if your body will cooperate on a given day. Or hour for that matter. Or if the pain will be so over-whelming all Maggie wanted to do was curl up in bed and wish for stronger meds. "Fibro fucking sucks!" she said aloud, startling the family of four standing next to their SUV in the space beside hers, the shocked faces of the parents apparent over the hood. A family who had remembered their towels.

"Well, this is as good as it's going to get," Maggie said more quietly trying to wipe the sand off a bit more with her flimsy polka-dotted socks as she slowly put on her shoes. She should have worn the ones that closed with Velcro. Her hands, today, could barely tie a clumsy bow on each sneaker. "I can do this. Anna is finally happy and that's what's important," she reminded herself as she slid her body gently into the car, waiting for the wave of pain to subside, then drove off, putting on her "I'm fine" face and leaving most of the sand behind.

The Color of Light

Rodney L. Lowman

Once, at the cusp of dusk
on the 37th floor of the
New York Hilton, looking
north and west to the Hudson River

past the flashing lights
of the MONY Tower,
I saw the
color of light.

Artists jabber on forever
about their need for it
but seldom speak
so all can know

their medium oozy gels
and watery shades
with which they
tell their tales.

Against sea or
even common trees
it forces their brushes
into action

soldiers reporting
for duty,
lathered up for battle,
light to canvas, sir!—ma'am!

As the light changes shades
the brush obeys,
re-routes,
adjusts the pressure

positive energy changes, then
reverses, now negative images,
hills and valleys appear,
complexity deepens

the artist's breath
rises, the brush quickens
and then it slows,
light having its way again.

And I, no painter, still
borrow from the reflective
California sun—
the wildest blues,

canary yellows,
persistent greens,
eye-piercing rays,
even from the fog—

the will to start again
each day,
words, not color,
on my palette,

compelled to look,
and then, to write.

Morning

Susie Parker

Sky blue after a gray dawn
Dolphin mobile with chiming bells and bright beads
Swinging slowly in the window
Sets a rainbow over the white sink

Distant palm fronds gleam
Sunlight shimmers the chrome faucet
Brings yellow tiles a glow
Steam rises from my coffee cup

Return to Harpswell

Nadia Harris

Often a sweetness comes
as if on loan, stays just long enough
to make sense of what it means to be alive . . .
—Stephen Dunn

My husband and I arrive in Maine after an eighteen-month absence. Soon after getting our second shot against Covid, we had brushed aside lingering misgivings. Masked and visored, wipes and hand sanitizer within easy reach, we embark on the long flight from San Diego to Portland.

We land in the early morning and drive straight to our Harpswell cottage. The sky is clear and I-295 is wide open. Everything looks the same, seemingly untouched by the pandemic. I want to believe that, find shelter from the daily deluge of Covid statistics. Peter, my younger brother, one of them, on November 19, 2020. I haven't yet made peace with the circumstances surrounding his death—in a Marseilles hospital, no family at his side.

We reach Brunswick in record time, drive past the pine grove bordering the Bowdoin campus and turn onto Harpswell Neck Road. It's a straight shot to our house. We'll be there within the next half hour. Fragrant air wafts through our open windows, carrying whiffs of freshly cut grass and pine. First on our right, then on our left, we glimpse the grayish blue waters of Casco Bay. Forsythias in full bloom lazily sway their branches to the stirrings of the wind. Right after the pond where the water lilies have yet to open, the Harpswell town marker welcomes us. We drive past the grange, the cemetery, the churches, the fire station, the school, and make a left onto our street. Following its meanderings, we dead end into our driveway.

Brilliant gold shoots sprouted from the tender green grass welcome us back. The pandemic has been good for the 2020 crop of dandelions. Last year, on the lawns of unoccupied houses, unhindered by human interference, the puffballs have sown their seeds to the four winds and completed their full life cycle. The result is stunning. Nature in all its exuberance. The strawberry patch too is in full bloom. This year's yield will be abundant. Under the Miss Kim lilac bordering the walkway, the grape hyacinths and daffodils have multiplied. They display a harmony of purples and yellows set against deep green clumps I don't recognize, all vying for their share of moisture and light.

Still holding my bag, I bend down to take a closer look. I count six leaves emerging from a crown anchored at surface level, six deep green serrated blades, their slender oval shape crisscrossed by fine streaks branching out of a median vein. With my right hand, I grab a clump at its base and tease it out of the dew moistened soil. It pulls easily, trailing a long thin thread that turns out to be part of an entire web of threads, each one sustaining its own clump. I have unearthed an underground network linking an entire colony of weeds. A breed unknown to me. They yield to my gentle pull, one after the other, till a sharper tug disrupts my steady tempo, severing the thread. A long string of runners is now dangling in my hand. I'll try again another time. More pressing work awaits.

Ed is already inside. He has unpacked the car, activated the septic computer, opened windows. I must go in and help. My feet are treading dandelions; I am breathing briny air. My eyes follow the trail of mist suspended above water. It will soon dissipate. The sun is already high above the horizon. I dawdle. Inside, cobwebs await, and two winters' worth of mouse droppings. It will take hours of cleaning to reclaim our home from intruding critters. Hours of housework interspaced with walks on the beach, the planting of vegetables, impromptu meetings with neighbors—*When did you get vaccinated? We've had our two shots; what a relief. How good to have you back; we missed you; we did too. Are your kids coming this summer? We are not sure; not all our grandkids have been vaccinated yet.*

It takes a couple of weeks for our resident chipmunk to make her first appearance. She leaps out of the stone wall and scampers away, dispensing with any sort of greeting. It must be an offspring of the pair that lived here in 2019. The parents would have remembered me. They may be dead. The average life span of a chipmunk is three years, I've heard. They survive as a species by being prolific—up to two litters a year, three to five babies in each litter. The one I just saw will be back. She'll want to take a closer look at me. Chipmunks are curious and friendly. I take out my phone to be ready when she reappears. I'll take her picture to send my sister. She used to love watching the chipmunks during her visits here. The pandemic and a recent Parkinson's diagnosis are keeping her in Istanbul this summer. Will she ever come to Harpswell again?

I'll need a caption for my picture, and it occurs to me that I don't know how to say chipmunk in any language other than English. I'll have to look up its French and Turkish translations. My French catalog of names of birds, mammals, trees and flowers is extensive. It was built through daily readings and dictations of literary excerpts that were part of the curriculum in the schools I attended in Istanbul. Yet, I did not always have a referent to associate with those names. They were words divorced from the things they designated; words reduced to their sounds. As for my nature-related Turkish vocabulary, it is limited to the names of flowers, animals and trees I encountered in the urban and suburban spaces I inhabited during my childhood and adolescence.

I share this problem with most multilingual persons. The range and field of our individual vocabularies do not coincide perfectly from one language to the other. The various contributing factors to vocabulary building—environment, experiences, interests—are not always present in equal proportions in the context in which we learn our various idioms. We thus end up with gaps that complicate our attempts at communication across languages. For me, this problem is compounded, now that, more and more, the drawers of my ancient memory stick and resist revealing their contents.

The French word for chipmunk is *tamia* or *suisse*, I learn. The latter appellation is used in French-speaking Canada, where chipmunks are natives. It stems from the black- and cream-colored stripes that mark their backs, reminiscent of those found on the uniforms of the Vatican's Swiss Guard. The word *tamia*—designating the genus within the *Sciuridae* family that includes squirrels and marmots—is used in France and other francophone countries where chipmunks don't live, except as imported pets. There are twenty-five species of chipmunks in North America and only one in Asia, the Siberian chipmunk, I also learn through my semantic inquiry. This explains that the Turkish word for chipmunk translates as "striped squirrel." It's a name Turks can relate to, given the fact they are familiar with squirrels, whereas their most likely encounter with chipmunks would have happened by way of the big screen when, as children, they entered Disney's magical world of *Snow White and the Seven Dwarfs*.

67

One morning, I open the door and there is a chipmunk perched on the granite boulder marking the top of our front steps. Hind feet planted on the stone, tail wrapped around her haunches, a green strawberry between her front paws held close to the chest, she is looking straight at me through white rimmed bulbous eyes, as if daring me to deny her the fruit of her larceny. *I'll gladly spare a strawberry or two, in exchange for a few moments in your company*, I want to tell her. Her defiant mien reminds me of my then two-year-old granddaughter, adamant about squeezing her own toothpaste onto her toothbrush while I attempt to prevent the waste and mess of blobs she produced the evening before. "Just a little bit, remember," I say, as she unscrews the cap. "Just a little bit?" she repeats, focused on the task at hand. She then presses thumbs and index fingers on the middle part of the tube, and out wiggles a long white worm she dangles under my eyes, a look of triumph painted all over her face.

A more distant memory follows, of Ayla's older brother Nico. It is early May, and our daughter and nearly two-year-old grandson are spending a few days with us in Harpswell. Ed and I have taken Nico out for a walk. It is a brilliant day; the air is crisp and clear. I point at the neighbors' crabapple tree in crimson bloom. I name it, and also each flower, bush and tree I recognize along the way. Near the top of the hill, from a crevice in the low stone wall surrounding the field of an old farmhouse, a chipmunk emerges. It positions itself on its hind legs, ears pricked up into perfect isosceles triangles, cream-colored chest palpitating. He is watching our trio make its way up and seems eager to meet us. "Look Nico, a chipmunk," one of us says. We stop for a closer look. "Look at his fat cheeks. He uses them as shopping bags. He can put lots of food in them to carry to his nest." Our eyes are watching Nico. His are on the chipmunk who, deciding he's seen enough of us, scampers away. Throughout the rest of our walk, like a mantra, Nico will repeat, *chipmunk, chipmunk, chipmunk.* He is several decades ahead of his grandmother in learning the name of the impish creature. Now fifteen, he maintains his lead in all things scientific, and many others besides.

After the long sequestration imposed by the pandemic and the uncertainty surrounding our projected family get together this summer, I find myself reliving moments from years past. Austin, not yet two, is standing on a ledge, watching the waves crash on the rocks. He is perfectly still and quiet. It is this little Londoner's first close encounter with the ocean. A few years later, I witness a similar scene featuring our San Diegan grandson. I walk into an upstairs room to find four-year-old Emil in front of an open window overlooking the water. He seems mesmerized. "I like to listen to the waves," he says, after a long silence. Those two scenes form a diptych in my memory, connecting my two grandsons through a shared poetic experience.

When I first notice the tiny yellow blooms on this year's cherry tomato plants, another scene replays in my mind's eye. It brings together, through shared mischief this time, two other grandsons, one who lives in London, the other in Vancouver. It was August and our tomatoes were slowly ripening. I had watched the fruits set and then grow into shiny green orbs, relishing in advance the taste of my first slice of vine-ripened tomato doused in olive oil. A cluster of three were the first to turn red and I was monitoring them daily.

One late afternoon, four-year old Nico and five-year-old Troy were playing baseball on the front lawn. I stepped out to watch their game, just in time to see Nico pitch and Troy bat the ball. It was pale red, a bit misshapen, the third of my nearly ripe tomatoes. The other two, marked with deep dents, were lying on the grass.

Harpswell is the scene of yet another infraction, this one committed by the adults. All of us are chatting on the deck while the children fish in front of the house. Suddenly, a chorus of "Aaaahhhs!" rises up from below, putting a stop to our conversation. "Jelani caught a big fish," someone says. They all come up in procession, the proud fisherman brandishing his trophy, brother and cousins in tow. It is the biggest by far nine-year-old veteran fisherman Jelani has ever caught. A striped bass, at least forty inches long. It will feed fourteen of us that evening, with leftovers to fill a few fish tacos the next day. Later, neighbors tell us that we were required by law to put the fish back into the water. None of us knew or admitted knowing at the time. There was too much pride, enthusiasm, and excitement invested in Jelani's feat, and too much pleasure eating the freshest and sweetest fish ever.

Lobster is on the menu tonight. After weeks of charting the rise of the Delta variant, of wondering how it might impact the travel plans of our children and their families, we are happy to be celebrating their safe arrival. Everyone is here except Jelani whose work is keeping him in San Diego. Two steaming lobster pots are waiting on the stove, another one is ready to receive the shucked ears of local corn. Ed, the one and only Maine native in the family, is the official lobster cook.

His audience will be smaller this year, when he plunges each lobster, head first, into the steaming water. Neither Austin, a disciplined vegan since starting university, nor Ayla, vegetarian and ardent promoter of vegetarianism among her elementary school friends, will be watching. Ed's cheer squad, now reduced to Nico, Troy and Emil, will be no less vocal, notwithstanding.

Everyone is busy. There is butter to melt, lemons to quarter, drinks to serve, the boiled lobsters to drain in the sink. The commotion surrounding the last-minute preparations of a lobster dinner ruffles me. It always has. I like to cook alone, in a quiet kitchen, without hurry. The kitchen turned beehive feels downright stressful this year. The extended confinement and slower rhythms our lives have taken these last eighteen months, together with the effect of advancing years may be the cause. The kids have noticed at any rate. I've been banished from my kitchen.

I make my way towards the deck. Two rectangular tables have been set, running its entire length. Each one holds crackers and picks, a big empty bowl that will serve as receptacle for the emptied lobster shells, stacks of paper napkins weighed down by rocks found on the beach. They've been smoothed and shaped by the swells to the plump round-ness of loaves of bread. There are platters of bean and tomato salad, of quinoa couscous, of watermelon flavored with red onion and mint, baskets of homemade rolls. Soon, we will be sitting down together to enjoy the food, the soft summer evening, the retelling of stories of summers past.

Eastward across Harpswell Sound, the reflected rays of the setting sun have painted a large swath of sky purple, rose and orange, and set ablaze the windowpanes of Bailey Island cottages. Our daily light-show, we call it. It will last a few dazzling minutes before its brilliance softens and melds into dusk. A billboard welcomes travelers as they cross the border from New Hampshire into Maine, and it reads: "Maine. The way life should be." In this very moment, for me, that promise is being fulfilled.

Together for Always

ShuJen Walker Askew

Lights, bells, and ornamented trees,
our family piled into the yellow Oldsmobile
for that much needed getaway in the open breeze.

We chased dust devils across lonesome deserts,
rode mountains that crashed into red skies,
and swam in the stars bursting across the horizon.

Oldies blasted on cassettes, like "I Heard It
Through the Grapevine" and "R-E-S-P-E-C-T."
We sang while Dad pointed out his past Air Force bases
and Mom's Taiwanese sausage fried rice filled our bellies.

Eight hours later we arrived at Station Hotel.
Mom disappeared at the blackjack tables. Sister and I, the arcade.
Dad, the couch in the high-rise room, overlooking
flashing lights shouting *Life* on the Las Vegas Strip.

When vacation ended, we dragged our bags into the car,
riding in silence, our faces glum with the return to school,
work, and household chores.

These years we traveled, summers and winters,
comforted us like skin from head to toe.
Our presence fed each other on that magical
journey until the day it transformed.

Our bags packed.
Mom, sister, and I, drawn to that yellow
Oldsmobile. We piled in, alongside dad's empty seat
impression, aiming for the open road.

On the Move

Yvonne Sherman

1.

In the spring of 2020, we are halted in a kind of suspended animation, which changes the way we work and communicate and live in the world we've created for ourselves. At the same time, we try desperately to avoid this dreadful disease called Covid-19.

There are inevitable changes and challenges throughout our life, some planned, some unexpected, coming like a storm on a summer day. Do we plan what route to take when the sun appears again, or wander aimlessly until we are rescued?

2.

My father always comes home a little drunk on Fridays, but this time is different; he decides he'll go out later. My mom tries to stop him, and I hear the argument from my room. I crack open the door and watch the scene at the top of the stairs. I'm afraid she might fall down the stairs as they tussle over the keys to the Chevy. My father is not violent, just a quiet and unhappy man; she keeps a hold of the keys, and he leaves. Somehow, he gets the car started—probably by hot wiring it. Being a mechanic and a service writer for City Chevrolet, he'd know how to do that. He speeds away and that is the last time I see him alive. Where is he going and why is he stopped on the side of the road where another drinking driver—drawn by the flicker of the flare—plows into the back of the Chevy and pins him against a guard rail, never to regain consciousness? No answer.

When the police arrive in the middle of the night and I hear the sobs of my mother coming from downstairs, even though I'm only eight years old, I know that our lives are changed forever. I sense my mother's sadness and see how she steels herself against the impact of this tragedy, and I vow to take responsibility for my life and try to be as little trouble as possible. Within a few months we move from Linda Vista to Normal Heights and start building our new life.

After my father's death, in 1951, dressmaking becomes my mother's stay-at-home full-time job using the pattern drafting and fashion design she had studied as a young woman while working at Ratner's in clothing manufacturing. She becomes seamstress to San Diego socialites. If you read the society page of the San Diego newspaper in those days, chances are you'd see one of her creations in the photos for the Charity Ball or other social events taking place. Her expertise is re-creating dresses from Vogue like one designed by Givenchy in 1954 for Audrey Hepburn—a knee-length dress made of pink brocade faille, with a bateau neckline, fitted bodice, and wide pleats from the back of the waist finishing at the hemline—now displayed at the Metropolitan Museum of Art. The challenge for my mother is to fit these designs on clients who will never have figures like Audrey Hepburn.

4.

Dance becomes my passion. After seeing *Singin' in the Rain*, starring Gene Kelly in 1952, I dance my way down the street towards home and maybe that's when it is clear that dance school is where I belong, and even though I've been tap dancing since I was five, I now beg for ballet lessons.

My mother finds the most professional dance school for me, and my classes are the highlight of each day. I practice tap steps under my desk at school, and at lunch I teach my girlfriends the five basic ballet positions. Many a late night is spent keeping up with my homework to avoid the only restriction I have from my mother, when she says, "If your academic grades fall, you'll have to cut back on dance classes."

5.

During the summer I turn fifteen, the dance studio becomes my second home. In exchange for taking as many advanced classes as I want, I spend the mornings with four-year-old girls teaching beginning ballet. I can hardly keep from laughing as I watch them toddle in wearing their little pink leotards and tights and tiny ballet slippers. They come rushing in and can't wait to tell me whose birthday party they are going to after they finish class. Taking in payments and answering the phones from the students or their parents also gives me business experience, which makes me feel kind of important.

I never tire of dance class and feel myself getting stronger and my technique improving every day. Ballet is my foundation, at the same time I'm learning tap, jazz and contemporary which is very important for success in musical theatre. Vocal lessons are also an important part of my training. After being discovered on a local radio contest—where I sing and dance to the song 'A' You're Adorable—sponsored by Boldrick's Fine Shoes, I'm invited to become a member of the La Jolla Opera Guild. My voice lessons are free and I play all the children's roles in classic operas. As a prize for winning the radio contest, I receive fifteen silver dollars—enough money to keep myself in dance shoes for at least a year.

I dance, sing, and act my way through high school and continue to San Diego State as a Speech Arts Major, playing the leads in the department musical productions. During the summers, I perform with Starlight Theatre in the Balboa Park Bowl where I progress from a chorus girl to leading lady. Moving, always moving, closer to my goal of a life in the musical theatre.

6.

After graduation, I move to Los Angeles and after months of auditions and rejections and working at The Broadway Hollywood at night, I'm finally performing in the Los Angeles Civic Light Opera production of *My Fair Lady* and an original musical by Meredith Willson, famous for the *Music Man*. Then I'm on the move touring in arena shows for Walt Disney Productions as Snow White and Mary Poppins and other beloved characters, traveling throughout the United States, Canada, and Australia while actually being paid to do what I love so much. An especially exciting time is dancing on the 1970 Academy Awards and on other television variety shows—even dancing with Gene Kelly—coming full circle from being bitten by the show business bug in 1952, while watching the man himself *"singin' and dancin' in the rain."*

I truly believe the scripture passage from Ecclesiastes 3 which reads: "There is a time for everything, and a season for every activity under the heavens." So, after thirty years—from the time I put on my

74

first pair of ballet slippers—I feel my desire for the theatre is fulfilled and I want to settle down. Using the other half of my brain I become a retail manager, take up tennis, and much to my surprise, I'm not too bad at tennis, but better than that, I marry the Pro.

7.

Here I sit in front of my computer, locked down and now at peace with the most tragic event of my life and grateful for all the joyful experiences thus far. I have faith I can break open my heart and share all the treasured memories kept safely there for so many years. I'll begin today, writing a memoir entitled *Return to Pepper Grove.*

I'll stay in motion by doing everything that exhilarates and inspires me like walking to the beach, reading, writing, cooking, dancing, and playing tennis. Fortunately, all these activities add up to a good recipe for retirement, and a perfect time to contemplate the great beyond— my next big move.

Apostrophes

Elliott Linwood

perfume, boulevards,
embers, zephyrs, bubbles, gum,
coin, flags, the unsung,
fleeting commemorations,
brimming with entanglements

Spool

Elliott Linwood

flirting eddies spoon
dreaming dandelion seeds
unraveling their clocks

Liars' Club

Clara Frank

Twenty young people were holding their breath in the neighborhood bar at the Liars' Club's quarterly gathering. I was tasked to tell a story that is hard to believe, but true—or a lie. If they should find that I'm lying, any member could call me out and the penalty is to buy a round.

Tiffany and I are off to our latest adventure, this time to Switzerland. Wanting to avoid crowds and stay on a budget, we decide to go to a little-known place away from the beautiful people. No Chamonix's Moritz or Zermatt for us, instead a resort called Anzer which was recommended by Phillipe who is Swiss. "My uncle owns a ski chalet there and will give you a discount," he says. It is near Geneva in the French-speaking part of Switzerland. We don't speak French, but who cares, everyone speaks English everywhere, right?

Wrong. "Ninety-five percent of visitors are Swiss with a rare French-speaking Briton," Tiffany is reading too late, as we ride in a shuttle from Geneva to Anzer. There isn't much time for reading. The spectacular views of snowy peaks are all around us with the milky slopes of Mount Blanc directly across. Ahead of us is a death-defying one-lane curvy road. We are going way too fast, desperately hold each other's hands as our feet keep trying to hit an imaginary brake pedal to no avail.

"Whew, that was close, but we made it without going over a cliff," Tiffany says as we unload at the Chalet. Maurice, the owner, a little man who could pass for Hercule Poirot, is very hospitable. He speaks no English, says he doesn't know Philippe in Los Angeles, *ergo*, no discount. But the small chalet is cozy, away from the village, just what we had in mind.

Next morning, we have a cliché ski day shown in the travel brochures, the sun shining, the temperature 3˚C (37˚F), no wind. Maurice has our skis and a trail map ready in the lobby and, after latte and croissants, we are off on the ski shuttle.

"There are a lot of Alpine trails," Tiffany says after studying the map and handing it to me.

"What exactly does that mean?" I ask.

"It's a combination of downhill and cross country, the best part of each; you'll love it."

The village is active with vacationers heading toward the slopes which are reachable on skis from the two small hotels.

"I like those hotels, maybe next time . . ." Tiffany starts to say.

"Next time?" I laugh, "are we coming every year?"

"Let's take the gondola to the top," Tiffany says, ignoring the wise crack.

Up there, the atmosphere is relaxed. People are sitting on deck chairs facing the sun, in no hurry to hit the slopes. We, however, don't linger, but start exploring. In the bowl behind the large sundeck, we find three single-seat chairlifts, long outdated by California standards. It's quaint and relaxing to sit on the chairlift by myself free to admire, in solitude, the snow crystals on the pine tree branches.

"The snow is great, slopes are good, and there are no lines," Tiffany yells when we meet at the bottom of the chair after a half dozen runs, "but let's try Alpine now." We find a trail on the map heading west toward a *cafeé* and we get on it. Alpine skiing is wonderfully different. The trails are narrow but slopes only slightly downhill; no turns are needed. I admire shiny specks like diamonds on top of the deep virgin snow in the woods. But there are some animal footprints, I wonder what kind of creature would have such large claws. Tiffany is way ahead of me, I better hurry. In the quiet, I can hear scattered sounds of her singing the chorus of *Ode to Joy*, loud and off-key.

"There it is," Tiffany shouts after a while, pointing to a hut with the sign *cafeé.*

"Doesn't look like much, maybe a cafeteria, but it's someplace to eat," I tell her as we lay our skis against the wall next to a dozen other pairs. Inside, a surprise.

"This is no cafeteria," Tiffany says as we quickly pull off our snow-covered hats and gloves in the warm room. Groups sitting at the tables look as comfortable as if they arrived by limousine instead of skis. There are white tablecloths, bottles of wine, relaxed conversation, a three-piece band playing soft music, and no one seems to be in a hurry to leave.

"My kind of place," I whisper. Tiffany just nods, trying to pull off her ski parka with the unexpected help of a young man who stands up from a nearby table. By the time I return from a short trip to the restroom, the two are in deep conversation.

"Judy, this is André," Tiffany says, "he is local, and guess what. He speaks English! He asked if he could join us, and I said, yes. I hope you don't mind."

"Glad to meet you. You're a rare find." I shake his hand.

"It's not such a great accomplishment," André says. "They teach it in the local high school, but most kids choose not to take it. Wherever you go in the world, everyone speaks French of course."

"Did I say something funny?" he asks when we laugh at this.

"So you actually live here in the village?" I ask.

André turns to me and I notice his big, brown eyes.

"Mine," Tiffany mouths.

Pretending not to notice the mime, he says, "I live in nearby Sion. It's about sixteen kilometers. I have a motorcycle and there are shuttles for when it gets colder. Tiffany told me you are from Los Angeles. Were you both born there? They say in Los Angeles, everybody is from somewhere."

"We were both born in Los Angeles, but my parents are from Taiwan, and Judy's from Hungary," Tiffany says. After the waiter takes our order André asks her to dance.

"I have ski boots on," she says, pointing at her feet.

"You can dance in your socks; nobody will mind," he says, and off they go leaving me with my glass of wine for company.

On the trail, they can't seem to stop talking. Well, they can't ski fast and talk at the same time. They can catch up. If not, I'll see them at dinner at the Chalet. It's already three thirty. I don't want to ski the steep face, and the last gondola down leaves at four. It's easy terrain. I can go faster. I see the lodge in the distance and can almost smell the aroma and taste hot chocolate. I should look at the map to make sure which way to approach it, but no time. Got to go faster, deep breath, and a final push. That's when the ground disappears from under me.

◇◇◇

I paused and looked around at my fellow Liars' Club members. Everyone appeared fascinated, including Tiffany, who probably wondered where this was going. Paul started to open his mouth as if to comment, but I took a swallow of beer and quickly resumed.

When I open my eyes, I find myself in a crevice, the bottom icy, the sides steep and covered with deep snow. I'm about 20 feet down with one ski on, the other nowhere in sight.

The gondola, I must get there on time. *Don't panic,* I tell myself. I take off my remaining ski and, cradling it in my arms, attempt to climb. And I fall back. Up the wall and fall back. I look around my surroundings. The narrow rectangular hole has four walls. There's got to be one that's not as steep. I try the other three, now without carrying the useless ski, but after a while, I can see that my attempts are in vain.

"Aide-moi," I yell, and the echo repeats it. "*Èéédééém.*" There is no response. I'm probably pronouncing it wrong. I almost laugh, but once again panic takes over. I keep yelling and circling from one wall to another as millions of large snowflakes start coming down mixed with a small avalanche my useless efforts had started.

It's getting dark when, finally, I see a shadow at the far end. I start rushing toward him in my heavy ski boots and stop in my tracks. He makes a sound. *Hurrr* and, again, *Hurrr.*

A bear! A brown bear covered with snow. I turn and run in the other direction. There is a shadow there, too. *Hurrr* and, again, *Hurrr.* Another bear.

I turn to run, but there is nowhere to go.

I drain the rest of my beer. Paul and Liz were exchanging glances but most of the others still appeared enthralled.

"Liar, Liar!" Paul yelled before I could say anything else. "There are no bears in the Alps. You have to buy a round."

"Not so fast," I said. "Although brown bears became extinct in 1904 in the Swiss Alps, they recently made a comeback. Several have been sighted in that very region. Google it. You buy the beer for calling me a liar on erroneous grounds."

"So, what happened?" everyone asked, once again surrounding me, holding their new beers purchased by Joe, as Tiffany handed me one.

"What do you mean?" I shrugged.

"The bears, what happened with the bears?"

"Oh, they caught her and ate her of course," Tiffany said as we quickly exited, taking our beers with us.

My Grandmother Dreams

Esteban Ismael

It felt up, rising—not like in heaven neither
here, but somewhat mile-high
like Denver, an airport with clean windows
full of light and crowded with people
in no rush. This is how a conversation begins
between her and the attendant at the kiosk
who speaks Spanish and verifies she is
a citizen because sometimes dreams choose
to mimic reality. Her older sister sits waiting
in the plane she is trying to board but the teller
is busy asking about passport stamps,
the shelf-life of ink pads, Deutschland
and Madrid, her place of birth beside a single oak,
the shine of cactus needles and fine dusts of Phoenix
that lingers in morning, or sizzling gold
grasses in the front yard at dusk.
A creek, watermelons humming in sunlight.
Her sister has been dead
over ten years but this doesn't bother her
for now and when the teller asks her if
she'd rather board a plane to a place
that translates into both heaven and sky
this beautiful woman says no, speaking
in English for the first time lucid
now more than ever

Editors' note:
Esteban Ismael's poem is placed here
near the center of this book
as his teaching is at the center of our workshops
and our love is sent to him from the center of our hearts.

83

Pulling Teeth

Nan Valerio

I got my first job when I was ten years old: pulling teeth.

The five- and six-year-olds in our Chicago apartment building trusted only me to help them remove their very loose but holding-on baby teeth. Their relieved parents paid me ten cents for each tooth I pulled from the willing child's jaw, as much as the Tooth Fairy would bring the tooth grower.

I was experienced, as I had pulled all my own baby teeth when they were ready. My brother, who watched my procedures, wouldn't let me near him. Our younger sister, however, was happy with any help she could get. But I didn't get paid for family work.

After a stint of hospital nursing and tech work in the glaucoma research labs, I married and had children of my own. The stoic oldest needed some help to carefully remove his first baby teeth, then usually continued on his own. The weepy second one, because of the "red stuff," which occurred along with the procedure, suffered emotional torment with each extraction. The third, Little Miss Me Too, couldn't wait to proudly join the older half and show she was a big girl now; she wiggled loose her own teeth.

Number four suffered the greatest trauma when her little brother inadvertently removed her first tooth. He raced down the hall to loudly alert his sister that their favorite aunt and uncle had arrived as expected. She ran out of her room on hearing the happy news. Heads met. Sister's top front tooth cut deeply into her brother's forehead, then the tooth fell on the floor. Loud screams and tears ensued. Grabbing the tooth, I saw that it was not fractured. I rammed it back into its space in her jaw and told her to hold it there firmly. A big Band-Aid, mostly for show, was applied to her brother's injured face. I checked that the tooth was in its socket, solemnly sheltered by the owner's hand, wet with her tears.

With a treat of ice water sipped through a straw and being cuddled by the visiting auntie, the wailing eased. For an entire year, the wobbly tooth remained in place. Finally, one careless bite at snack time sent the tooth to the Tooth Fairy envelope and placed under her pillow. Other teeth required mom's help, with few tears shed.

As for the youngest, we hardly noticed the loss of his teeth, given the continuing commotion of four older siblings, many friends coming to play, and school activities. When a tooth came out, only sometimes with mom's help, he made sure it was retrieved by the Tooth Fairy who properly paid for it.

None of my eight grandchildren lived near enough for this experienced tooth extractor to demonstrate her well-honed capabilities. When the grandchildren announced a tooth being loose, grandma would remind them of a major purpose of the young tongue, to wobble free then flip out that baby tooth. Grandma sewed and mailed a Tooth Fairy Pocket to assure the appropriate financial transaction would occur.

It's All About the Teeth

Linda Smith

When I was six years old, my baby molars had to be removed. They were full of cavities, not from saccharin in Tab—I wouldn't start drinking those until I was 12—nor sugar in the Canada Dry ginger ale Grandma gave us, no, just from general neglect.

We arrived at the clinic, me and Mom, bright and early. The dentist put what looked like a baby elephant's trunk over my nose and mouth, but it was just a way of filling me up with ether. He told me to count to 10. I got up to maybe seven and was out.

I dreamed of a Mother Goose world where all of the characters and animals were in a sort of square dance circle. One by one, Mother Goose called each animal into the center to gaily dance a bit with her. My turn was next and I heard her calling, "Linda, Linda, Linda." I never got to dance because the surgeon was waking me up. Wanting to tell him all about it, I opened my mouth to speak but couldn't get any words out because as I later learned, my mouth was full of bloody cotton.

I still remember that day in some detail. Afterwards I rested on the wooden bench, worn yellow in places from years of people sitting and leaning on it in this clinic. When it was time to leave, Mom and I took the clickity-clackity El to the Frankford Street Depot and boarded the first 59 bus home. These green and cream-colored "buses" were called trackless trolleys. Their long roof antennas contacted overhead wires, but they ran on wheels.

◇◇◇

When I was 12 years old and lost 22 pounds between February and May, the boys started to clamor for my attention and thought I was a "new girl" at school. My transformation was so dramatic as I came into full bloom in more ways than one, they seriously did not recognize who I was. It was a fun, party-filled spring and summer. However, September began a series of Wednesday afternoons in Dr Einhorne's dental chair. It seems my mouth was again full of cavities. Which is really too bad, he said, with such straight white teeth and a pretty smile, you could have been a toothpaste model. Huh, I thought, just like that, another career down the drain. And I whooshed my mouth with water and spit out blood.

<><><>

When I was 18, I woke up with excruciating pain in my glands and ears. I thought a highway was going through my mouth. It frightened me and made me wonder if something was fermenting inside, preventing me from swallowing. My gums and everything having to do with my head except my eyes hurt, so I called Dr. Einhorne. Come in right away, he said. Oh, looks like you've got some impacted wisdom teeth here. You'll need to see a specialist and he sent me off to his friend, the specialist.

The specialist confirmed, yep, all four of 'em, impacted all right. When would you like to have those taken out young lady? Tomorrow, I said. He laughed. How about next week? So the next week I went and had all four of my impacted wisdom teeth removed, and in a different wing of the same hospital, my (sometimes) friend Laurie's mother had a hysterectomy.

A bunch of our friends had been to see her mom and then came to see me. I was out cold. The first thing I saw when their talking and jostling woke me was Laurie (who did actually go on to do some modeling) pointing and laughing at me. Turns out I had blood-stained gauze hanging out of my mouth, and she said it looked like I had walrus teeth. Ha-ha-ha, I thought, that's hilarious. And then my mind wandered off to how Laurie always had to take control and make a situation about her, and I questioned whether anybody would have even come to visit me if her mother hadn't been in the same hospital. I was jealous and resentful of her at the same time.

But it was nice to see everybody, and they came with little presents like a stuffed bunny and crayons and a coloring book. My friends were wacky but mostly sweet. It was the '70s. There might have been drugs involved.

Breathe

Katherine Porter

I can't breathe
he gasps, the cop's
knee unmoving upon
his crushed neck
his gasps unheeded.

We can't breathe
they scream, as police
shoot teargas and rubber bullets
at kneeling protesters
armed only with signs.

I can't breathe
she coughs, the virus
clogging her lungs
with her own body fluids
a lonely death arrives soon.

I can't breathe
the teenager yells
his worry for his future
on a pollution filled, hot planet
where no one may survive.

I can't breathe
my daughter struggles
her spontaneous collapsed lung
a reaction to smoke
from catastrophic forest fires.

Why can't I breathe?
I ask, when
my biggest burden
is not knowing when I'll be able
to do what I want to do.

But I can't breathe
I shout, when the weight
of racism and devastation
rains down to where
I comfortably sit.

Take a deep breath and act
I declare, from my throne
of white privilege
doing anything is better
than nothing.

With a kind heart
and arms open
I must do something
or this

may be

my

last

breath . . .

Me and Mexico

Georganna Holmes

I have been to Mexico,
to Rosarito, Ensenada,
dined at El Rey Sol
(and suffered upset tummy after).

I've been to Tijuana
When it was little more
than a dusty mud puddle
sprinkled with tourists.

I've seen Mexico City's
strolling musicians,
broad tree-shaded avenues,
Anthropological Museum,
Centro Medico for visiting orators
and disruptive Cuban dissenters.

I've been to Puerto Vallarta,
Cuernavaca, Taxco . . .
and a little fishing village
on the Gulf of Mexico
so crowded we had to overnight
(well-fortified with gin and tonic)
on a damp sandy beach.

¡Ay, caramba!
I have been to Mexico.

Tough Women

Elon Mangelson

1.

The women I know who passed their share of genetic material embedded in my cells were not the weak or fragile who complained about their lot or lost their way when life served up adversity. None were the type to berate the fates of misadventure. They rose like sphinxes from the ashes of their trials to become more beautiful.

They were tough women.

2.

I saw her once from what I can remember. I know there was one other time because of Mom's favorite four generations photo. I was a chubby baby girl sitting on my mother's lap, and two older women stood smiling behind us.

But this time I was seven. She was silver-haired and bent with age, shorter than my mother and grandmother who settled her into a chair. I am sure I was encouraged to reach up and kiss her cheek because that is what our family did.

Two memories linger over time: the feeling of reverence and protection from those who helped her. I knew she was someone special. The other was of her reminding my mother not to forget the salt in the tapioca pudding she was preparing for our dinner. I was told she was my great-grandmother, Becky. There were no more visits because soon she was not with us anymore.

3.

In Colona Diaz, a religious Mormon colony in Mexico, Becky and her family made their home. The colony's inhabitants were immigrants from the United States. It was around 1912 and Becky was a contented, if busy, mother with fifteen children and a farm to run. Everyone pitched in. There were eggs to be gathered, cows to be milked and taken care of, cheese to be made from the creamy milk, and crops to be grown and attended to. Her husband Charles was often away. He was appointed as legal counsel for Diaz as well as the other six Mormon colonies with the Mexican government. It was a good life.

Recently, however, the colonists felt unrest in the country. There was a revolution brewing. Suddenly, one day in July, the news raced through the town—Poncho Villa, the revolutionary who saw all Americans as enemy, was coming. They must evacuate now. With fear in their hearts, Becky quickly gathered her children. No thought about what they were leaving except to set free the animals that needed to fend for themselves now. Meandering pigs and chickens were adding to the confusion. But safety for the family was all that mattered. They put whatever would fit into their wagons and headed for the United States border. In a few hours Becky went from a life of security to a penniless refugee.

This was a critical situation for those she loved. It was a time for action not a time for tears. Becky had her large family to comfort and care for. As a member of their religious group, she encouraged them with faith. They could have gratitude for the government-issued tent over their heads and rations provided to eat. No time for regret. Just face today and trust to the future. Though a picture of privation, it was not long until even in the tent city there was guitar music and singing in the evenings.

4.

It was about two and a half years since the exodus. For a while, Annie, Becky's oldest child and my grandmother, with her two plump little babies and adored husband Elmer were sharing Becky's modest house in Thatcher, Arizona. Earlier after leaving the tent city, they all homesteaded for a time, but Charles and Becky decided it was best for their children to be near other families and have access to better education. The Mormon Gila Academy was in Thatcher, and Charles managed to rent a home for them there. It was a plain wooden house with no insulation, but with wood floors instead of dirt and a separate pantry shed in the back. It wasn't large, but a welcome improvement over the tent days. Annie and her family occupied one bedroom and Charles, Becky and her younger children were on the other side of the house.

Annie kissed her sweetheart Elmer goodbye that morning. How excited they both were. Annie's life was about to change again. Tomorrow they would move to their own little home near where Elmer would be working in the fields. He would be close by and they could be together each night with their two little ones. She could even look out the window and see him working. At her excitement, he laughed as she handed him his lunch box, "Can you wait just until tomorrow?" He threw her another kiss and rode off.

Everything was packed and ready to be loaded in the wagon. The hours sped by with songs of a new life singing in her head. But oddly, that afternoon, Annie saw the workers' wagon return and watched as it drew up at her door. Lying in the bed of the wagon, paralyzed on one side and robbed of the power of speech, was Elmer. Drenched in disbelief, dreams in shards and her beloved husband helpless in their bed, what was she to do? It wasn't really a question—whatever was necessary. No time for self-pity with those who needed her so much. Gone were the dreams, but now she would hope for recovery. When things seemed impossible and Annie felt her feet slipping from beneath her, Becky was there for courage.

Annie's quick wit and sense of humor found laughter even in hard circumstances. She always tried to let Elmer only see her smile. At two or three years old, little Enola—my future mother—set herself as language instructor. Placing both chubby hands on his face, she told Elmer, "Papa, say Ma ma, say Ma ma." When Elmer's efforts met her satisfaction, she would shriek with joy as she ran to her mother, "Papa said Mama, Papa said Mama!"

5.

Time weaves a tapestry of change. It nudges us along until one day in surprise we see its footsteps in our lives. Enola had left her childhood days behind and was now a grownup with a husband and children of her own. The heat of an Arizona town in the desert had given way to their home in Utah.

Enola agreed and supported the plan but she knew it wouldn't be easy. Born in a refugee camp just across the Mexican border, she realized she grew up never thinking life would be easy. Maybe that made the rewards better. It was the early 1960s and she and her husband Leon were looking ahead. Finances were tight now with nine children. Their needs would only increase as they grew older. Leon had already purchased some farmland and started a small dairy to augment his teacher's salary at the local college in their small central Utah town. If he returned to school and earned a PhD it would be harder now but increase his earning capacity long term. At his age and with nine kids they both knew it would require an immense sacrifice

That was how Enola found herself caring for the home, a plethora of kids, the family's large vegetable garden, a dairy, and an alfalfa field that needed irrigation to keep it alive—all with an absentee husband. Of course, it was only with the help of the older boys, who were to carry the load of the outside work that it was at all feasible. They must be up before the sun was fully awake to milk and feed the cows, get ready for school, and make it on time. Then there were lessons to be done and again cows milked and fed at night. Surely these teens needed some time for fun. No wonder sometimes they complained. It was a lot to ask. Still, she was the adult responsible to get it all done. Unhappily, even with her best efforts, things did not always go well. Exhaustion walked beside her. Even more difficult were those days when the throbbing of her head assailed her every effort, a malady beginning in early childhood. There was no time to rest.

Somehow the years passed and graduation day did arrive. On that special day, my father insisted my mother don his cap and gown while he took her picture. For, he said, she earned the degree as much as he had.

6.

Unique experiences shape each generation. I have never been driven out of my home by vigilantes or had a stricken loved one delivered to my door. I do not have fifteen children or even nine, but my own seven have been my schoolmasters. They have taught me about my inadequacies and been my motivation to do better. They are white boards with messages telling me when I am off track and helping me find the way back. I had the good fortune to be let loose on earth with my own field of boulders so I could learn to plant flowers around them. Sometimes the boulders grew to be mountains requiring climbing ropes for survival and spiked shoes to traverse their shear faces.

7.

I once had an ecclesiastical leader ask if I were resilient. "Have you had enough trials and hardships in your life?" Without a moment's hesitation I answered yes. Immediately there welled up inside for starters, the demise of a four-decade relationship and being turned out of my home in the housing bubble collapse a few years back. The truth is, however, it is not how many trials we have but what we choose to do. It is this choosing that determines if we mount up from the ashes of our trials ennobled with new strength and solicitude, a light to comfort others with their loads to bear. May I be the conduit to pass on this legacy of strength from those who came before to those amazing women who will follow—tough women for the generations ahead.

The Best Bed Partner

Susie Parker

They do not snore.
They do not hog the covers.
They do not poke you with elbows, knees, or anything else.
They support you, no matter what position you take.
Undemanding, always at your side.
I am, of course, referring to pillows.

Ode to Purple

Nancy Foley

You are
Lavender and lilacs in early Spring
Woody wisteria teased by the breeze
Elegance, splendor, grace

You are
Jacaranda blossoms falling like snow
Morning glories or clematis climbing the fence
Royalty, dignity, strength

You are
Violets, gladioli, potted hydrangeas
Cosmos, petunias, juicy plums
Passion, privilege, power

But the pandemic pushed you into posing
as most restrictive tier

You have become
A bruised eggplant, sour grape
Weeping onion, dried-up prune
Suffering, sorrow, stress

You are labeled
A toxic foxglove, wilting iris
Punch drunk pansy
Flying purple people eater

You will reign again one day
As most beloved shade
Oh, purple mountain majesty
For all your faults, I love you still.

The Storm Drain

Walter Besecker

Billy struggled to lift the iron grate. "Come on Jake. Give me a hand. It's too heavy for me."

Jake was slow to respond. The other boys looked timidly at one another and were silent.

"Come on Jake." Billy was irritated. "You gotta help me."

Jake hesitated, then knelt opposite Billy. His knees sank into the wet, soggy leaves and soaked his pants. *My mother's going to kill me.* Jake clenched the cold metal bars with both hands. Despite the cool fall breeze, Jake felt a warm rush sweep through his body as he strained to lift the grate. Both boys moaned under its weight. Slowly, the iron grate loosened and, like the lid of some long-lost buried treasure chest, broke away from its earthen prison. The boys slid the heavy cover to one side. Jake's hands and arms ached. *This isn't a good idea.*

Billy sprang to his feet, excited about the adventure that lay ahead. "Now we have it."

"Hey guys," Billy's voice rang with excitement, "who knows what might be down there? No one has ever crawled through there before. I'll bet no one ever thought about doing it either. We'll be the first."

"Where does it go?" Jake mumbled with trepidation.

"I think it comes out by the small creek behind the high school," Billy said with a tinge of uncertainty in his voice. He caught himself and his self-confidence once again took control. "It really doesn't matter, does it? Wherever it goes, it's going to be a fantastic experience."

The timbre of Billy's voice set him apart from the other boys. It was an older voice, one that conveyed authority. Although only a little older than the others, Billy had experienced much more than they could dream of in their short lives. He had traveled the world with his parents. He was given much more independence as a child than any of his followers. His embellished tales of travel, finding his way when lost, and other courageous exploits impressed his peers and captivated their imagination. He commanded their attention when he spoke. The boys listened to him. They would follow him anywhere.

"Is everyone ready?" Billy asked.

Sam raised his arms and responded with an enthusiastic "Yes." He was the only one.

Without saying another word, Billy dropped into the open concrete pit. His feet were nearly submerged in the decaying black muck that covered the floor. His new sneakers were ruined. "I shouldn't have worn them," he said under his breath.

The time for regrets had passed. If his parents knew what he was up to, they would have stopped him immediately. *I'm glad I made each one of the guys swear not to tell anyone what we were doing today or where we were going. Someone would have stopped us for sure.*

"Get your flashlights out and ready. It's going to be dark in there." Billy barked like a drill sergeant as he surveyed the cramped quarters. The storm drain entrance was just a few inches above the liquid sediment on the pit's floor. It was smaller than he had anticipated. Billy examined the tunnel and saw that, after fifteen feet or so, the grey concrete pipe that led away from the pit curved to the right and was no longer visible. Billy imagined that it might wander underground like a maze. The idea of a maze and the challenges it would present only heightened his excitement.

The concrete storm drain was barely large enough for his shoulders to pass through. It would take a bit of maneuvering to position himself to enter the tunnel, but it was possible. He knew that once they were on their way, there would be no retreating.

The pit had a foul odor, much like the rotting potatoes that Billy once found in his grandmother's cold cellar. The air was motionless around him, despite the breeze that blew the dead leaves from the trees above. It was late afternoon. They'd have to hurry if they wanted to finish this bold exploration before supper.

"I want everyone to keep up with me. No room for slacking off." Billy said. "Jake, you come in last. I need to know that all five of you are accounted for and you're the strongest besides me. Let's go. There is no turning back once we go in. Everyone has to keep moving forward."

The boys fell into line. They looked at each other. No one protested. It was too late for that. Billy was their Pied Piper leading them to an uncertain destiny.

Billy squatted and entered the narrow, dark concrete storm drain. It was too small to crawl on all fours. He dragged his torso forward by using his arms and legs like a soldier crawling under barbed wire fences, whom he had seen and idolized in movies. His imagination ran wild. He traveled only a few feet beyond where the storm drain curved to the right when total, absolute darkness surrounded him. He moved his hand in front of his face. He couldn't see it. Exhilaration and brief terror raced through every pore of his body. He tightened his grip on his flashlight. His fingers searched for the small button that would once again give him sight. He pressed and the tunnel was saturated with a crisp sharp cone of light.

As Billy shifted the beacon back and forth, shadows created by the furrows and debris took on a life of their own. Billy regained his courage and moved forward with renewed determination and speed. He could hear the voices of the boys becoming fainter as his distance from them increased. There was no room to turn and look. He relied on the sound of their chatter to estimate their distance behind him.

The storm drain's twists and turns were not what Billy expected. He swiped at the spider webs and pressed against the side of the drainpipe away from the decaying leaves and garbage that obstructed his path. The smell of unidentifiable decaying animals caused him to retch and hold his breath for long stretches. The voices of the boys trailing him became a faint cacophony as they, in turn, encountered the odors and debris. Billy could only smile.

In places, the tunnel walls glistened with tendrils of green, like the veins in polished marble he had seen on the columns of large cathedrals in the city. These tendrils grew thick and coated the walls with a slick layer of discharge seeping in from the surrounding earth. The discharge pooled on the floor. His hand slipped on the glistening mass as he attempted to move himself forward. He recoiled from the slime now covering his fingers and palms.

Small, swarming insects bit his wrists, arms, and face, and irritated his eyes. *Who would have thought anything would be living down here?* He moved more quickly to put the pests behind him. He could hear the muffled protests of the boys far to his rear as they, too, were confronted by the pests that lay in their path.

Billy's enthusiasm and energy intensified as he advanced through the tunnel's curves. The voices of his followers grew more distant.

After several long moments, he paused. He could no longer hear their voices or movements.

The beam of Billy's flashlight grew dim. He realized he had been in such a hurry to begin this expedition that he forgot to check the batteries. He called to the boy he believed was next in line behind him. "Give me your flashlight." There was no response.

Billy's light expired. Once again total darkness engulfed him. He could see nothing. He heard a rustling ahead. It wasn't the wind. There was no wind, no breeze here. The air was stagnant. Something was moving, sloshing through the damp leaves, brushing aside the twigs, moldering paper and empty plastic bottles that covered the storm drain floor. The patter of small feet grew louder.

"Give me your light!" Billy screamed.

Roundup

Lloyd Hill

I look like a bandit from an old cowboy movie,
blue bandana covers my face, ready to rob a bank,
or a cowpoke going to herd cattle, masked for grit.

What can I give the world today, as my lasso twirls
around jackrabbits and tumbleweeds? On desolate trails,
eyes of passersby hard to read as mine try to smile.

What will the world give me today? Hopefully not Covid-19,
the curse of 2020, keep your distance partner. Look
but don't touch, with college classes cancelled lots
of time in my bunkhouse; questions with no answers.

Trees, flowers, and alley bazaars take my mind away
from whirlwind thoughts: work, write, walk, get dead
tired so I can somewhat sleep, stay here and now more
real than Georgia O'Keefe art, perfect Easter lilies with
their green stems and yellow pistils in furled ivory cups.

Jasmine now wafts aromatherapy, bird songs, brighter days,
I'm a different person in April 2021, two Moderna doses
down, weary and saddle sore from busting broncos all year,

a little wiser, a little more paunch, but onward ho, we've beaten
back some bad hombres and I feel like a blue-ribbon winner. I've
traded my bandana for a surgical mask—the Joe Biden look.

Enhanced Zoom

Frank Primiano

Maisie sat alone in front of her laptop, frustrated. She made audible the expletive that had been pounding in her head for the last quarter hour: "Son of a bitch!!"

Vocalizing such an extreme profanity, while with others, wasn't an option for Maisie who took pride in projecting an unflappable, kindly, granny image. However, her doctor was clear. Internalizing strong emotions was a major factor contributing to her sky-high blood pressure he was unable to control pharmaceutically. "Stay calm or you could run into real trouble," was his admonition. So, to let off steam when by herself, she indulged in the luxury and recuperative power of uninhibited swearing.

The reason for her present ire was her inability to join a Zoom meeting with a trio of her girlfriends. All four were mature widows, living alone. Since the pandemic began, they took Dr. Fauci's advice to heart: self-isolate, social distance, and wear a mask. Thus far, the group had avoided infection by minimizing their contacts, not only among themselves, but also with their respective extended families, especially their darling rug rats. No more hugging the grandkids for a while, maybe never again.

The ladies' get-together via computer every Thursday morning was their primary social engagement of the week. But the meetings were becoming mundane. They could discuss only so many geriatric maladies and bemoan the state of the country and world for just so long before their conversations became repetitive.

Maisie's internet problems were due to age: not hers but her computer's. It had a built-in microphone and camera but was slow. She didn't replace it because of a limited budget.

Today, Maisie was sure she followed the same steps she always did to join the group, but the process stalled. Her image on the display looked back at her while she waited for the host, Sarah, to let her in. More than fifteen minutes since the meeting began and still no admittance.

She decided to call Sarah on her cell to ask about the problem when the screen blinked. A message appeared under her picture: "Enhanced Zoom" and "Yes" and "No" with a checkbox beside each choice.

What's this? Maisie had never noticed these words before. Had Zoom been updated? Nothing else on the screen appeared different than usual. *Maybe I have to click on "Yes" to join the meeting. Might as well try it. Been waiting long enough.*

Her face joined those of her three friends, all framed in separate squares. The "girls" were in a serious discussion about something but stopped before speaking in unison, "Hi." "We'd almost given up on you." "It's about time."

"Well, I'm here at last," she said, peeved at the rebuke, knowing it wasn't her fault.

The three went silent and stared with wide eyes at her. In response, Maisie gawked from one image to the next struck by something strange: all three of the women were wearing masks over their mouths and noses . . . for a Zoom meeting.

"What's up?" she asked.

Sarah didn't mince words. "Where's your mask?"

"What do you mean? We don't need a mask on the Internet."

"Did you choose 'Yes' for the Enhanced option?"

"Yes. It was the way I joined the meeting."

"Didn't you read the instructions that appeared when your cursor crossed the word, 'Enhanced'?"

"No. I just hit 'Yes'."

"Well, you should have read them. Get a mask and put it on immediately. No questions. Just do it."

Maisie, confused, reached for her KN95, and hooked the elastic loops over her ears.

"Good," Sarah said, watching her adjust it.

"What's going on?" Maisie asked, concerned.

"My son-in-law, Brad, was here yesterday when he got a call about an emergency at work. He went for something from his car, downloaded an app onto my computer, and used it to connect to his office. He was in a hurry when he finished and said he'd be back in a few days to remove his changes from my computer."

"So, things worked out?" Maisie asked.

"Yes and no," Sarah said. "As I explained to Mary and Helen, before you joined us, the app Brad downloaded is an upgrade to Zoom called Enhanced Zoom."

"Oo-kay," Maisie said.

"Enhanced Zoom has a special feature, which Brad's company needs to run its business. It lets any computer admitted in an enhanced meeting to transport small amounts of matter to the other computers in the meeting."

"Wait a second. That's crazy," Maisie said, trying to make sense of Sarah's explanation. "Even I know you can't send something physical over the internet."

"We thought that, too," Mary said.

Sarah cut back in. "It isn't crazy. Brad works for a chemical company. They set up Enhanced Zoom meetings to transmit powders, liquids, and gases among locations. That's what Brad did with the stuff he had in his car. He sent it to their headquarters."

"I don't believe it." Maisie shook her head.

"I didn't either, but I watched him do it. His boss got the sample instantly."

Maisie thought awhile before saying, "Really? That's too amazing."

"Yes, it is," Sarah agreed. "But don't you see the downside? It negates the reason we use Zoom. We're no longer isolated. Material can pass amongst us during our meetings."

"Are you sure?" Maisie asked, becoming uneasy. "Even through my old, barely-working computer?"

"Brad said the age and make of the machine don't matter, as long as it has an open USB port."

"So that's why we're wearing masks?" Maisie asked.

"Not entirely," Sarah said. "When we opened the meeting, Helen blurted that she had been exposed to an unmasked Trump canvasser whom she opened her door to without thinking."

"Yes," Helen said, interrupting. "I had a Covid test but the results haven't come back yet."

"As soon as I heard her story," Sarah said, "I had the three of us put on masks. You weren't alone in ignoring the warning. None of us had taken it seriously. So, Mary and I may have been exposed to Helen's exhaled particles. Unfortunately, before you put your mask on, you, too, may also have been exposed to particles that could have lingered in the air near Helen's computer after she exhaled them."

Panic gripped Maisie. She seized one of the ubiquitous bottles of sanitizer placed strategically around her home and doused her hands before slipping one under her mask to soak her lips, nose and chin. Her breathing increased noticeably.

A ring tone sounded. Helen said, "That's my phone." Her image disappeared from her square.

"So how do you feel?" Maisie asked Sarah, her voice tremulous.

"Alright, I guess. I've coughed a few times, probably because my throat's dry from talking."

"How about you, Mary?" Maisie was looking for assurances. "Are you worried?"

"I might get tested in a few days if I don't feel well."

This did nothing to calm Maisie whose anxiety was making her sweat.

Helen's face reappeared on the screen. She dabbed at her eyes with a tissue.

"What's the matter?" Sarah asked in full concern mode.

"My test was positive. I have the virus." She began to sob.

"Oh, no," Sarah said.

Mary followed with "Dear God."

Maisie was scared, more for herself than for Helen. Panic. Her heart rate took off. Breathing became difficult, more like gasping. *I could die from this.* That realization sent a bolt of fear and anger through her body. "Motherfucker!!" resonated from deep within her being.

Her friends were aghast. They'd never before heard anything like that escape refined Maisie's lips. The three stared in alarm at her image. It stared back, wide-eyed, gasping, each breath concaving her mask, taut, across her wide-open mouth.

Helen shouted, "That's enough, Sarah. Stop . . . now."

Startled by this command, Sarah called out, "Maisie, are you okay?" She continued more slowly and quietly. "Relax. You were right. Material can't be sent over the Internet. There is no Enhanced Zoom. Brad programmed my computer to let me display that 'Enhanced Zoom' message. It's all fake."

"The three of us wanted something to liven things up," Mary said. "Our meetings have been so dull lately. We decided to trick you for some laughs."

"Don't worry, Maisie," Helen joined in. "Everything's fine. I don't have Covid. You aren't in any danger. It was a joke we pulled on you."

Sarah removed her mask. Helen and Mary removed theirs also. The three were smiling.

"We're sorry if we frightened you," Helen said. "We only wanted to have a little fun."

The three pranksters beamed at Maisie. Her image peered back at them, eyes still wide, unblinking, mask still in place, head supported by the back of her chair. Her body jerked twice as the last of her agonal breaths followed the same path blazed by her final pair of words.

Knowing

Dave Schmidt

I'm sitting in a theatre viewing an action drama
With a cop in pursuit of a thief down a side road
By identifying with the officer who is doing his job
Can feel the excitement during the long chase scenes
I Am Aware

I desire to fly while seated in my dream-world,
Lifting off from the ground, levitating through air
Then to rise above the trees and tallest buildings
Feeling free as my ascent takes me above the clouds
I Am Lucid Dreaming

I'm driving down a busy street, cars on both sides
And stop at the light, move ahead on a green signal
Then notice a cop in my side and rearview mirrors
Observing the fear arising from my emotional heart
I Am Mindful

I reach another stage of sleep toward early morning,
Can view one dream after another entering my mind
There is a sense of having a body but cannot move
Later exit that stage and the control of my body returns
I Am Witnessing

Bouncing Through History

Tim Calaway

Took a tumble down the large stone blocks,
a kindly medic wrapped my injured head.
Gaze through the gauze at quaint old Giza
and imagine how the city looked
in the days of Pharaoh long ago.
Was the climate back then so hot?
Dried remains could attest to that, or
was it a paradise of honey
and dates? What drew people to settle
here along the river, their picture
language telling fantastic stories,
with birds, beetles, and kohl-lined eyes abounding.
And such wonderful tales they do tell,
if whoever it was who chiseled
the Rosetta Stone can be trusted.

The Great Bicycle Marathon,
A Summer to Remember

Keith Cervenka

As kids, who didn't look forward to summer vacation? It meant play-
ing baseball, building forts, hide-n-go-seek at dusk, and . . . playing
baseball. Our Central Illinois neighborhood, which was full of baby
boomers, often gathered at the corner of Rosemead and Winnebago,
down the street from my house and across from the Smiths, and their
ten kids.

There were four of us hanging out one day, when Paul Smith men-
tioned a bicycle marathon.

"What's a bike marathon?" I asked.

"It's in my *Guinness Book of World Records*," he said. "Some kids
in Indiana rode a bike for fourteen days."

"How do you do that?" Star Malpeade asked. We nicknamed him
Star because he always tried to take the extra base.

All eyes turned to Paul. "The bike has to stay in motion, never
stopping."

"Twenty-four hours a day?" I asked.

"We can beat that," said Jim, Paul's younger brother. He wanted to
change his name to Cleon because he thought Cleon Jones, of the Mets,
had the coolest name in baseball.

The more we talked the more we thought we could beat the record.
So, nine of us had a planning meeting. Two would take turns riding
four-hour shifts, while the next two riders waited nearby to help with
emergency bike repairs. Star volunteered his red twenty-four-inch
Schwinn that we stripped down to its bare essentials, keeping only the
reflectors. Repairs had to be made while the bike stayed in motion, so
we needed clear access to the tires and chain. For a couple of hours,
we practiced rider exchanges, chain replacement, and changing front
and rear wheels.

"I think we're ready," said my good friend Jim Blessington, who
had a crush on my younger sister, which I didn't understand.

We had no starting pistol, no band to cheer us on. Just Paul on the
bike and eight boys in the middle of Winnebago Drive, waiting for him

to push off and start our quest for greatness. We watched as the bike turned right on Rosemead for its first of many trips around the block.

We made it through the first night and the next day without incident. By the afternoon, kids milled about my front yard while parents gathered to get the latest bike marathon news. There was a buzz throughout the neighborhood as all eyes waited for the latest exchange. At the top of Winnebago, Star pedaled toward Chris O'Neil who stood ready to take over. Star swung his leg over the seat traveling faster than he should. Chris trotted alongside trying to match the speed. Star let go of the handlebars thinking Chris had a hold. He didn't. The bike tumbled to the street and became motionless except for the spinning back wheel. Young and old who watched let out an audible gasp. Star hustled to pick up the bike then walked it forward.

"The back wheel's still spinning!" Mr. Etter, my next-door neighbor, who was my dad's age, yelled from his driveway. "I think you're ok."

There was no rule book, no umpire. Just our sense of right and wrong. After long debate we called it off. We had gone only nineteen hours. Deflated but not defeated, we talked about how much we had learned in those nineteen hours.

A taller bike would make for easier repairs, so we commandeered Stephen Smith's twenty-six-inch flat-black Huffy. We even stripped off the reflectors this time. We practiced an easier rider exchange, collected spare tires, innertubes, chains, pedals, wrenches, everything we would need, all laid out on my driveway. We even pitched a pup tent in the front yard for guys to sleep in.

A crowd gathered around the bike as Paul readied himself for the restart. He shoved off, coasted down Winnebago turning right onto Rosemead. He waved to neighbors who had come out of their homes to watch the restart. They waved back wishing him luck. Now, all we had to do was break the record.

We made it through a week and that's about when excitement turned to boredom. Guys rode out of the neighborhood just to get a different view. My dad plugged a portable TV into our yard lamp. Midnight to six a.m. was the hardest. We listened to rock-n-roll on WIRL, talked Cardinal/Cubs baseball, and freaked out over strange sounds we never heard before. I swear, we heard a baby screaming one night. Turned out to be a cat in heat.

WIRL Radio showed up one morning and recorded an interview with me and two other guys. They played that interview all day long. A reporter from the *Peoria Journal Star* stopped by that day while a group of us were hanging out in my front yard. He pushed aside an expensive looking camera that hung from his neck, asked questions, and jotted notes on a pocket-sized spiral notepad. With his back toward the street, he didn't see Greg O'Neil ride by, standing stiff-legged on the pedals, giving us his goofy grin trying to make us laugh. We maintained our serious, "I'm being interviewed" expressions and continued answering questions.

Suddenly, from up the street, Greg shouted, "The chain broke!"

I looked up the street and saw Greg walking the bike. "What do you do now?" the reporter asked.

I bolted for the driveway, grabbed a spare chain and a screwdriver, then ran toward the bike. Paul and Jim lifted the back wheel high off the ground keeping the front wheel on the street and in motion. Greg clutched the handlebars guiding the bike while I replaced the chain. The reporter kept up, snapping photos as Star and Brian Karsten walked alongside hoping to get in the frame. An article, with two pictures, appeared in the next day's paper. We were now famous. The bike marathon was the biggest event to ever hit our Rolling Acres neighborhood.

"I just heard something I don't like." Paul said looking concerned. "There's a couple guys who want to stop the bike."

That got everyone's attention. "We only have four days to go to beat the record," said Steve Bobbitt who looked a lot like Rod Stewart. "Who would want to do that?"

"A buddy heard a couple older guys from the other side of the creek talkin' about it."

"Do you know them?" I asked.

"I know who they are. Said they're driving over here tonight."

There was a voice from behind. "They'll drive by my house first, Keith, before they get to yours. If I see a car that doesn't belong, I'll whistle." It was Tom Cullen. He had a stocky frame with a military style haircut and a no-nonsense attitude. We were told he's the one who called WIRL and the *Journal Star*. "Tell the rider to pedal to another neighborhood soon as you hear my whistle."

We transferred the tents to my backyard and moved the tools and spare parts into the garage. By ten o'clock all the kids had gone home.

Mr. Cullen sat stationed on his front porch. We kept the radio off and our voices low. Jim Blessington rode the bike nearby, while Paul, Brian, and I sat on the curb in front of my house, listening and watching. An eerie quiet had a grip on the neighborhood. In the darkness, only the sound of our muffled voices could be heard.

Then, just after midnight, we heard Mr. Cullen's whistle that everyone knew. He used it to call his daughter, Dori, in at night.

Paul yelled, "Get out of here, Jim!"

Jim pedaled as fast as he could up the street and around the corner heading to the far end of the subdivision. Slow-moving headlights appeared down the end of the street. Then the hum of the engine as a dark Chevy Chevelle rolled under the streetlight. It continued its slow drive down Rosemead past Winnebago and out of view. We all took a deep breath.

"Was that them, Paul?" I asked.

"Not sure."

"If they keep driving down Rosemead, they might see Jim," Brian said.

"They won't find him." I said hoping I was right.

Headlights again, this time from Keenland at the top of Winnebago. It's the Chevelle. They had just gone around the block.

"Oh, God," I heard someone say.

They stopped near the corner. I saw the glow from an inhaled cigarette. The headlights turned . . . heading toward us. The car picked up speed then slowed to a stop in front of us. We got our first look at them through the rolled down window. I'd never seen them before.

Karen—My Neighbor

Chi Ping Hu

Karen moves in with her 85-year-old mom, suffering
stage three cancer, and 29-year-old adult son
as our new neighbors. One early Saturday morning,
when I leave to teach Chinese with my elementary school son
follows, after a brief introduction with her smiling
face and a simple exchange of "Hi!" on the sidewalk

her shirt looks like the vibrant jacaranda flower tree
planted in her front yard, in full spring blossom
popularized as Serra Mesa's flower, the purple color
turns the air into a lavender veil under the afternoon sun
on my way back home, I see
the petals falling with ease from a spring breeze
like snowflakes floating in midair
landing on her green, green grass of home
serene—such a beautiful unforgettable scene
only, if only she has no worries or responsibility
else they are blown away daily

An accountant at a Japanese insurance company
a nurse taking care of her sick mother
a mother providing for her son
who sings country at a Pacific Beach Night Club,
inheriting the same profession as her ex-husband
we rarely cross paths due to different schedules

yet I can see life is hard on Karen,
but never hear her complain,
on the contrary, I may hear mother and daughter
chatting, laughing, talking on the phone, enjoying country music,
watering plants and having occasional family gatherings
with many visitors, but never get out of control
Fruits, veggies, and herbs branch into our yard

through an old wooden fence.
Several times I think it's raining,
but as I peer through a small gap in the fence
it's only her hose watering roses.

These happy noises disappear after she loses her mom
and the saddest thing in her world
happens one year later,
she buries her son—saying goodbye one last time.

Later, she returns to us a borrowed wheelchair
and gives me a bulb of amaryllis and rents a moving truck
to begin her weeklong journey
back to her hometown in Murray, Kentucky
many pots and plants are left behind in her front yard
as if leaving all memories in California.

One day during the pandemic, as the bulb blooms again,
she calls with good news
she will marry her high school classmate, Bill,
and sends a picture of her front walkway at night
repaved and reconstructed by Bill's hand
with colorful gemstones carefully adorning the edges
crafted by an artist in love

I cannot help but feel joy for her
after many years of sorrow
her wedding gown and ring's color
just like jacaranda flowers

The Red Shoes

Susheela Narayanan

We are in the middle of dinner when Father puts down his spoonful of curry and rice and asks: "What shall we do for your birthday this year?" I stare at him in startled amazement. Is that a twinkle I see in his eyes—my usually stern-faced military father who rarely smiles? My tenth birthday is coming up in a few days. I am excited but not that much; we do not usually celebrate birthdays with cake, balloons and loads of presents, as many people do today. Maybe mother will make a special dinner, with "payasam" (a dessert made of sweet milk, vermicelli, and nuts).

"You like Chinese food. We'll go to Nirula's for dinner," he decides. Nirula's is a very posh and well-known Indo-Chinese restaurant situated in Connaught Place, the main circular shopping center in New Delhi, known for its fashionable restaurants and stores—a place we visit only on special occasions. "And would you like some new clothes?" he asks, surprising me further. I have just read a story by Hans Christian Andersen about a little girl who has been gifted a pair of shiny red shoes that transform her life. (Only later will I realize the tragedy of that tale.) In my imagination, I am that little girl with flying pigtails who twirls around excitedly in her red shoes—I so desperately yearn for those shoes! My father smiles again when I tell him what I want and the next day we go to Bata's, a premier store for footwear located in that very same shopping center. With much pomp and staid gravity, the salesmen parade an array of shoes before me until we finally find a pair of red leather Mary Janes that fit me like a second skin. I go home with joy in my heart and on my face as I parade around the house in those shoes and show them off to my mother.

On my birthday we go to Nirula's—I proudly wear my red shoes—but I cannot remember what frock I was wearing. We sit in the more cosmopolitan Continental section and order sweet corn and chicken soup, followed by fried rice with chicken and vegetables, and my favorite egg rolls on the side. The pièce de résistance is the dessert, Peach Melba, which I now think is some kind of flavored vanilla ice cream with sliced peaches around it and—this is the best part, a thin wafer stuck in the middle. I eat it slowly as I savor the smooth cold treat on my tongue! I am not allowed to eat ice cream often so it is a very, very special treat.

For many successive birthdays, I got the same red shoes (my size changed every year), until I outgrew dresses and switched to wearing more formal Indian style clothes in college. But going to Nirula's for dinner and eating Peach Melba remained a family tradition as long as we lived in New Delhi and became inextricably entwined with my memories of my father. Later we moved to Bangalore, and I subsequently got married and moved to Canada, but my father would continue to take my younger cousins, and later my children, out to dinner to similar restaurants regularly—he loved the company of young children and watching other people enjoy the same foods that he did!

I visited Nirula's in New Delhi, fifty years later with my teenage children. It is now transformed into a noisy popular joint mainly frequented by a young, college crowd and serving pizza and other modern delights. There is no Peach Melba on the menu.

How Long?

Mary Thorne Kelley

Theme from the 2nd Piano Concerto
by Serge Rachmaninoff

How long a night can be!
I cannot sleep—I yearn for you
so helplessly.
And if I doze, a nightmare rends my peace—
again I see you depart
without even a look or a word.

How short a joy can be!
One moment's bliss—we join and kiss—
and then must part.
The many times I've heard and felt you say
how much you loved and missed me
now become such a dear memory.

How long a month can be!
I wait each day throughout each week
for news from you.
When many weeks pass by without a word,
how deep my heart sinks in fear
that your love for me may disappear.

How long a year can be!
As months have passed and times have changed,
have you changed too?
How long must we stay thus so far apart?
Or have you found a new love
who has taken my place in your heart?

How long can this life be?
Am I thus doomed to yearn for you
eternally?
How can I soothe my heart its aching void?
How long must I bear your silence
while I wait for you how long?

Office Aquarium

Jean E. Taddonio

Seemingly unaware
of their confinement
unlike me in this room
they glide as if water
was their wind
and they, stringless fish
like kites flashing colors
silent, shifting
chasing bubbles.

These angels lull me to peace
while I wait and pretend
there is nothing to fear
behind those doctor's doors
both the ones that say enter
and the ones that say exit
unaware of why I'm here
or why I'd rather be
somewhere else

Having a Ball with Balls

Angely Gonzalez

The word "ball" is mostly known for the object we use to participate in sports and games. We know that they roll, bounce, twirl, fly, skip, turn, and curve. They do these different things based on the sport we are playing, how the ball is made, and how the player uses it. If thrown in a particular way—putting a spin on it as pitchers do, they curve deceiving the batter expecting to hit it. In handball, there is another deception—cutting the ball—which is done by striking it with the side of the palm as one is hitting it against the wall. This causes the ball to spin, surprising the opponent. Many times, a hit that cannot be returned. Knowing how to use balls helps us play a better game. In bowling, for instance, there are reactive balls and non-reactive balls and they vary in weight. When a reactive ball is fitted to one's hand structure and swung strategically onto the lane, it causes the ball to slide and curve. Whatever sport we are playing, we always hope the balls land where we intend them to go and achieve the goal of earning the points. I enjoy most athletic activities involving balls because they are all different.

A bowling ball is carried with the entire hand and the correct weight must be selected in order for it to be manageably swung as a pendulum and thrown onto the lane. A glove is sometimes worn for a better grip of the ball. A handball fits in one's hand allowing it to be cradled with the palm slightly open. It can be thrown and hit with a bare hand—it weights a few ounces. A golf ball is round, has little dimples on all over, and is hard as a rock. It is small enough that one can hold it completely in one's hand, but it's so hard that it must be hit with a metal club.

Ball, of course is a funny word with multiple meanings. The other day, I participated in a Best Ball Golf Tournament, and we had one player missing which allowed each one of us to be able to hit a ball twice at whichever hole we wanted to. There were two ladies and one man. In one of the holes the man hit two balls and each of the ladies hit one. After the first shot, we went to search and approach the balls to determine which of the balls was closest to the pin to take the next shot from. As I got closer to the balls, I yelled: "I can see Marty's balls. They are lying next to each other." All I heard was laughter. I am the enthusiastic excited one in the group and I see them smiling often as we play together. This time when I heard them laughing hard, I wondered where the humor was in what I said. Then I realized and I laughed, too. It was funny. Thankfully, this was not a work environment nor was I playing with coworkers because my comment could have been interpreted as sexual harassment. Imagine that? That is not what I meant when I said having a ball with balls.

I am fond of participating in sports and recognized that although I had never thought about it before, there are many times when I have heard myself and others talking to a ball for it to do what we want it to do. When I talk to my ball, I say: "go in baby, you can do it"— asking it to go into the hole; or if it hits a bump and rolls, I listen to myself directing it to keep rolling to get more distance. I hear myself telling it to go left or right or straight. In bowling I tell it: "come on baby curve, curve" so that when it approaches the pins, it hits between the one and third pin for a strike to occur. And yes, I have heard myself say "no, not that way." Of course, the ball is just doing what it is intended to do and going in the direction I send it to—even if I think the ball should know where the final destination is.

I talk to whichever ball I am playing with because in my mind I think the game is between the ball and me. I think I am actually encouraging the ball and coaching it for top performance. Someone suggested I should give the balls names and I thought it would be a good idea; but then I feared that if I did, I would be going a little too far. I can just imagine me calling one Sassy, Bitchy, or Bouncy, and people paying attention to my conversations with them. They for sure would think I had lost it—not the ball—but my mind. Whether I name them or not, we are the team. I want to tell my ball: "good baby— good ball. You are a good ball." I want to start saying: "I am on the ball with my ball, and I am having a ball with my ball." After all, without the ball I wouldn't be focused on what I am doing and I wouldn't be having fun.

I see the balls in the air, on the ground, on the lanes, on the courts. I can hear them when I hit them and when they bounce. I rub them clean when they need to be cleaned, and I put my initials and draw little hearts, smiles and stars on them; and although I cannot smell any particular scent from them, I do have a good feeling of satisfaction and pleasure because I am playing with them. I wish I could say I smell and taste sweet victory out of playing with them, but that is not always the case. Whether we win or lose at playing with balls, let's always remember to have a ball.

Remember When

Rodney L. Lowman

Remember when there was no virus,
when Corona was just another aging
beer? Like when we only had Joseph—
the angelic one—before the

arrival of Marta, the screamer
who made *us* scream until the
neighbors called the cops and
when, after ten straight nights

of it, we secretly wanted her out
of our lives. We would take
door number two because not
even hell could be this bad.

Like when the dinosaurs still
thought—if they thought at all with
their dinky brains—that they were god
until the gods said, enough of that.

Once nothing we did,
we the chosen ones, was
bad enough to get us or those
who came after us whacked,

we who lived in the city on the
hill in that obscenely big white
house with the glare problem. Back
when titans boasted with their stuff

and thought they could last
forever if not them, then their
kin, and we all bought into it,
green-eyed, but still hopeful.

Like when only poor countries—
ain't it sad—had to suffer and we,
with our view and our stashes still
knew we were the favored ones

Like when they named all the
other planets and galaxies, not
caring that they already had
names, but would not likewise

name their own—not even
their star—just earth and
sun because—well, just
because they could.

If you were the god, you'd
be pissed too. You or your
engineers screwed up on that
one. Even you had to see

the design flaws—all that
hubris with those big
brains. Soon they would
be wanting your job.

You'll give them one last chance.
a hundred thousand earth years
perhaps, but you'll re-angle
Jupiter just in case.

Cement Makers

Jean E. Taddonio

they rumbled through the night
with their weighted power
pouring liquid rock
on the gardens

doing their best
to silence the flowers
that weren't to their liking
hoping to ban them forever

they said to themselves
how dare they share
the same space as we
who know all right and wrong

men made of rock don't know
that even dandelions bloom
and push themselves
above stone

through those blessed cracks
a sign of hope
those mighty weeds
whose flowers persist living

oh foolish men who think they are
all-controlling gods
can't they see the strength and beauty
in a garden full of color

when will they learn
the damage they churn
for an earth built of fear and strife
they too will lose the little they have

if they don't stop now
if they don't stop now.

December 9th, 1967

Manuel (Manny) Pia

It was just before midnight, and I was standing in front of the Greyhound bus terminal at the Pickwick Hotel in downtown San Diego. A mixture of anticipation and apprehension churned in my gut. I had made the most important decision of my young life by deciding to join the U.S. Navy, even though it totally wasn't my choice. I had received my draft notice for the U.S. Army and didn't want to end up in the jungles of Vietnam.

I was nervous about going to boot camp since I lived a half-mile from the San Diego Navy Recruit Training command. That would be like being in jail with your home right across the street. Through the fence that surrounded the base, I had seen the recruits incessantly marched, disciplined, and handwashing their clothes from buckets of cold water. It freaked me out to the point I told my recruiter. He promised I'd be sent to the other Navy Recruit Training command in Great lakes, Il. A Chief Petty Officer, he stated, "Because it's winter, they don't march or drill because of the snow. You only go to classes to learn your sailor skills. They even send your laundry out to be washed." I was relieved but still doubted that was exactly true.

My mom had dropped me off, and I had pitifully complained about not wanting to go, but she wasn't listening and told me to get out of the car and "go become your own man." A single mom, she had strived my entire life to be my nurturer. I knew that night wasn't easy for her, but later she said it was the best advice she ever gave me. I sighed and entered the bus terminal.

The bus terminal was dead, with only a few tired-looking travelers hanging around, a shoeshine guy asleep at his stand, and a bored ticket agent at the Greyhound window. He took my government voucher and handed me a ticket for the Express to Los Angeles. Less than 30 minutes later I was transiting north on I-5 and looking out at the lights on Point Loma. I held my Navy enlistment packet tightly on my lap.

I knew I would be away for at least three to four months. I had never traveled out of California, which made me a little homesick, but eager to go someplace I had never been. I tried to sleep but couldn't.

We arrived at the bus terminal in LA about five in the morning. The place was a hive of noise and people, far different from San Diego. The confusion worked on my anxiety, but I pushed out and walked ten long city blocks to the Armed Forces Examination and Entrance Center. It was an old, grungy office building which looked eerily foreboding. As I entered, I was amazed to see hundreds of young men standing around trying to figure out where to go. They ranged from those who protested the draft with their peace signs and "give a shit" attitude and others, like me, just trying to get to the right service window.

At the Navy counter, a sailor in dress blues grabbed my packet, ripped some papers out, added some others and shoved it back to me. He shouted, since the discord of voices was deafening, to follow the RED line which was painted on the floor.

"Don't drift onto the YELLOW line or you'll be drafted into the frickin' Army."

For the next five to six hours, I felt like I was on an assembly line. I was probed, poked, and had to answer numerous asinine questions, like what political party I affiliated with. Cripe, I wasn't even old enough to vote. I was passed from one military functionary to another, yet the weirdest part was when the medical types made fifty of us stand in a circle and drop our shorts and spread our cheeks.

"Any of you gentlemen fart, I'll send you straight to Vietnam tonight," the doctor stated. No one farted.

At the end of the examination, I was shuffled with a group of men, and a few women, into a large empty room.

Some military officer had us stand in rows and said we were making the most important commitment in our lives. He swore us in, then said, "You are going to serve your country as enlisted personnel. Always be proud of your service."

At that moment, I was honored about my decision, especially when I swore, ". . . to defend the Constitution of the United States against all enemies, foreign and domestic; that I will bear true faith and allegiance to the same . . ." It made me feel so important. I was going to become part of U.S. history.

The Navy recruits were then moved to another room with chairs, and a TV that didn't work. We were talkative, being emotionally stirred by our swearing in. I joined the recruits flying out to Great Lakes, sitting on one side of the room. Another group, being bused down to San Diego, sat on the other. I started up a lively conversation about what it would be like at Great Lakes. I felt exhilarated and reassured, then the rug got pulled out from under me when I heard someone shout my name.

"Pia! You're in the wrong damn group—get your ass over here—you're going to San Diego."

Shocked, and slightly numb, I mumbled something about my recruiter and a promise.

"What promise? If his lips moved, he was lying to you."

An hour later, I was on a crowded bus heading to San Diego—and back home. Just before midnight we entered NTC San Diego through gate 6 off Rosecrans Street. Two nights before, I had been with my friends driving on Rosecrans, lamenting my leaving. I was deadened and couldn't believe it. I thought of ways I could kill my recruiter when I got out of boot camp. We drove up to a building designated Receiving and Outfitting and were herded off the bus and told to grab anywhere to sleep. The place was packed with new recruits, all of us clueless with what came next. I ended up sleeping on a stencil table—with no blanket. Tired, pissed off, and slightly scared, I wrestled to fall asleep. I just kept obsessing at my current predicament. "What the fuck did I just get myself into?"

Wearing His Pith to the Plinth

Hilary Walling

Wearing his pith to the plinth
My father, Englishman George, set out
Confident in his proper riding attire
That in 1930, Britain ruled the world.

George knew not what sat upon the plinth
Maybe Queen Victoria or good King George
And so with the Indian sun beating down
George felt sure that he reigned supreme.

Nearing the plinth he doffed his pith
In honor of who might stand there
And as he gestured his respect with a bow
He beheld the statue of Vishnu.

A bronze figure on a lotus flower
Surrounded by a crowd of worshipers
The British monarchs might rule the world
But to the Indian people ruled by Britain
It was Vishnu who ruled the universe.

Oxford Dictionary Note:

Pith—Short for pith helmet.
A light hard hat, made of dried pith or cork and
covered with cloth, worn to give protection
from the sun in very hot countries.

Plinth—The stone base on which a column or statue
stands. Used since 1592.

131

Forest

Susie Parker

Moonbeams
Sunrises
Spirits
Imaginary worlds
Home
Wilderness inspired
High violin tones
Glinting silence
Combination gorgeous
Trees themselves

My Ears Are Weary

Michele Garb

As a young girl they weren't weary, but then I started wearing that same old shaggy dress. Paraphrased from *Try a Little Tenderness* by Otis Redding.

At the age of twelve when I got the disheartening news that I needed glasses, my self-image was forever altered, and my ears bore the burden. But they were young strong ears and they could take it. Bravely they learned to fearlessly carry their cargo everywhere.

As I aged, glasses came and went. Thicker and heavier they got; however, my plucky ears were always up to the task. Then there was the time gremlins stole through the house at night and cunningly shrunk the font size on all my pill bottles. After that I had to get bifocals and still my ears carried on.

Regrettably there was more misfortune. I could cite the day I learned of the need for hearing aids although it actually was discovered quite earlier. The previous times I just didn't hear it. So now there were two items jockeying for space on my ears. Do the glasses go over the hearing aids or under? I'll never know, yet my ears took everything in stride and figured it out.

Hearing aids are interesting at doctor's appointments. When I first got them, it took me a while to be on the lookout for the ear thermometer during the appointment. I was already used to and not even thinking about my hearing aids by the time I had my first non-hearing related doctor's appointment. The nurse came at me with the ear probe and forgetting about the plastic plugs in my ear, I turned my head to give him better access. When he saw my ear, he did a double take and backed off, giving me a look as if to say: Why is there something in there? Don't you realize you are in a doctor's office! That is our special place for putting things! How am I supposed to do my job with people like you plugging up their ears?

Things only got more complicated with the pandemic; my ears have been called on for triple duty as they try to wear glasses, hearing aids, and a mask when out of the house. Again, things can get dicey at the doctor's office. After my first run-in with the previously mentioned

133

nurse, I have learned to be on the lookout for an ear probe coming at me. I am quick to remove the hearing aid before offending doctors or nurses looking for their "special place" to put stuff. I have mastered the art of removing my hearing aid while leaving the mask in place. Getting dressed again seemed to work fine with everything that had been taken off, going on over the mask.

Or so I thought. However, the physics of the situation had positioned the mask ear strap under the hearing aid. Once back in car, the face masked no longer needed, is ripped off. Ripping off the face mask, with its elastic ear straps, had put one of my hearing aids at the end of a sling shot, and I could hear it ricocheting off the doors and windows of the car. Since I was in a closed vehicle when it happened, I did not need to waste time searching the area outside the car, during the 20 plus minutes it took to find my $1000 hearing aid. It had settled beneath the front passenger seat, in a gap in the carpeting.

Yes, my ears are weary with their burden of glasses, hearing aids, and mask all jockeying for position behind my busy ears. Still, tiredly, they have been soldiering on. Then one day, ears fully encumbered, my cell phone rang and I held up my Air Pod, wondering where to stick it.

I heard my ears say: "You know where!"

Sonnet to Nature

Dave Schmidt

Nature awakes, a glorious vision
Flora and fauna, colorful display
These sensations to enrich cognition
Much to enjoy and learn, for all our days

Fields of multicolored flowers abound
Throngs of birds and bees swarming in the sky
Myriad plants to grow freely from ground
Above a gaggle of geese flying high

Deer dart abruptly at the slightest noise
Along and across meandering stream
Other creatures alert and maintain poise
Creation in harmony, pleasant dream

The maya of nature, reflections in . . .
Kingdom of consciousness that lies within

The Awakening

Rodney L. Lowman

I am asleep,
I am awake
I am somewhere
in between.

I am cocooned in
gauzy white sheets and
layers of blue and red,
light still in the wings.

I am betwixt
the Lucullan night
tended by an army
of invisible servants

and the dawn, when the
help abandons me to do
whatever it is they do on
their daily day off.

Soon I will be the boss again
I have not yet accepted command
but I have not rejected it either.
soon, but not yet, not now, not when

so many things are possible,
when a poem can be seeded
a story or book imagined
a trip or a new life sighted.

For now it is like an Uruguayan
vacation during our winter,
where my dreams tend to go—
the soft dunes of El Pinar,

searching for whales in
the tiny towns of La Rocha,
the sands wind-smoothed,
people happy with their fates

breath stolen in Punta Ballena
on the fragile steps of the chalky
Museo Casapueblo, gaze affixed
on the crested white sea.

For now, all things are possible
and none must I do, only the
need, briefly, to give up control,
practice perhaps for the final time.

Alligators

Lawrence Weiner

Inspired by and referencing: "Bats"
            —by Lawrence Coates

. . . a single perfect pearl of water.

Down about Louisiana, every man carries alligators in his pockets once the spring thaw awakens bats at the headwaters of Northwestern Ohio. An egg tooth breaks through its shell; restless alligators crawl out on the banks of wallets, cellphones, coins and combs, coil around keys, toothpicks in their teeth, nod in naps that snore while melting snow slowly drifts down the Mississippi. Gators slog in their pocket's shadowed depths, dream of crawling amongst the moss-covered cypress, tupelo gum, and swamp maples that syrup the bayous. Inner lids close over red eyes, block the steamy air rising from a low country boil. Searching through the muck, the bayou spreads clawing alligator toes in fresh soft silt and tickles long wide snouts of three thousand teeth. Thick dark skins begins to stretch.

Early Sunday mornings they catfish in to prey. The parish men pat their pockets to settle the alligators switching about their long tails; they gather in congregations, walking on water that, once fresh, runs into estuaries to meet saltwater and saltgrass for deliberation. They breathe in pews, watching the clouds swim above, grey, white, and yellow-bellied, a collection in hats against a short quick sin—a preacher's boat, as if heaven comes from alligator skins—unwillingly surrendered.

Men don't put their hands in jean's pockets drinking holy water down by the water hole under Breaux Bridge, in chinos on the lily pads of Houma, in shorts at the Shadow, Queen of the Teche, or in Sansabelts at Lafourche, Gauche and Bartholomew. The quick hand avoids alligator's cruelly delivered bites, but death rolls await the unsuspecting fools' hands that reach where they don't belong. Alligators growl in those pockets, easily keeping their mouths closed when pressed.

A reflection off the bayou, a double-bright orange shot of sun, rises like the waking water, sends high-walking alligators quickly down to hunt, or balancing twigs on their snouts to lure in a winged quarry. Early bats whoosh amongst half-drowned trees—the soft whiz of wings dip—lips parted for a pearl of water, where flights end in a single perfect snap of teeth. A catch put away for days, thrashed chunks of rotting flesh: ripped, torn, swallowed and savored in morning peace.

If the men about Louisiana are told they carry alligators in their pockets they laugh at the obvious. They'll show instead their glistening boots, belts, and sheaths—pat their bellies after lunch—pointing back where that morsel was prepared to enjoy thoroughly. They'll burble on about record setting lengths, secret nests, and wrestling greenbacks onto a pirogue without spilling beer.

But when summer sweats, the men let their alligators dance. The bellow of songs call out in chorus. They turn out their pockets, that hard, fierce, grey-green monster. Alligators, with crocodile smiles. Alligators that know what it takes to live, that know what scutes feel like to sleep on. The men's skin thickens, and claws reach as they blink inner lids. They slide into the water as the creek spills out a little faster, swelling up the rivers, flooding over; in pockets alligators shift, already hunting for August's sweltering heat.

Plato's Wife

Lloyd Hill

We learn and gain from outside entities.
Cats, dogs, and husbands all offer wisdom

oftentimes lost. Losing is an art but
gaining is not artless. The poet Sappho

said bird songs informed her writing
before her star rose. Husbands not so

finely domesticated offer insight into
the untamed human animal we hear,

so we listen. Plants communicate—
Jasmine tells me sex is in the air.

Mediterranean sand and seaweed speak
through my toes. Listen as you sip wine,

the grapes are talking to you. Attention
to the outer helps still the inner and offers

a love of wisdom or *philosophy,*
that led to my widely acclaimed

Cat & Dog Wisdom Poems that further
led to my husband's *Dialogs,* the smash BC

bestseller. For these we thank Hera & Zeus
for their continual inspiration and wisdom.

Mary Lee, Tyrant Reformed

Norma Kipp Avendano

Harry finished his OD (Officer of the Day) duties, slept four hours, and then we drove 400 miles from Parris Island to La Fayette to spend Thanksgiving 1946 with my parents. It was also my mother's thirty-ninth birthday. There, I discovered that Mary Lee had become a four-year-old terror, undisciplined and rude, talking back to her parents, and doing and eating as she pleased. Mama, looking tired, was clearly re-signed to Mary Lee's tyranny. Daddy thought it was hopeless.

"Let me have her for a while," I offered. "She has both of you wrap-ped around her little finger and it's not good for any of you. I promise you she'll be a changed child when we bring her back."

"You got that backward," Daddy said. "You'll be the changed one. You don't know how stubborn she is, just like a Georgia mule."

I knew because I had heard Mary Lee say, "If I cry long enough, I get my way." And I knew I could hold out against her unlike my parents who must have grown tired from raising the rest of us with harsh discipline. Discipline that had paid off. Mary Lee was being raised differently and nobody was happy with the results. Before leaving, I took Julia aside, the sister I loved from the moment of her birth, the one with the great brown eyes and gentle ways. "Wait until summer and school is out," I whispered, "then we'll come for you."

Three weeks later on another whirlwind weekend trip, a trans-formed Mary Lee was returned home. She was saying please and thank you, taking afternoon naps, smiling and laughing instead of scowling, eating properly, and her chronic constipation was corrected. "Why, it's a miracle," my parents marveled. "How on earth did you do it?"

"With a lot of patience," I sighed, "and a set of rules we both followed. I gave her choices and held her to them and didn't give in to her whims and demands."

"And I'll bet a lot of spankings," Tommy said.

"No, never." Mary Lee in my lap pulled my head down to whisper, "Tell 'em 'bout when you made me stay in my room."

"Are you sure you want me to?" I whispered back. Mary Lee agreed, then hid her face behind her hands. "All right, but remember it

141

was your idea." And to the family, "I was wrapping your Christmas presents with Mary Lee watching. When I finished, she came over to the packages and began kicking them, splitting the paper. All my work for nothing. I asked her why she did it and she pouted, 'because I wanted you to play with me and you wouldn't.' I told her she had just lost more playtime with me and sent her to her room until Harry came home. When he walked through the door, she ran to tell him of the surprise record I had for him, but she talked so fast he couldn't understand."

Looking down at Mary Lee's upturned face, I added, "Good thing he didn't, Miss Priss, or you might have gotten that long-deserved spanking." Mary Lee buried her face in my chest, then stole a look at her parents. Everyone laughed except Mary Lee; she cried, wanting to go back to Parris Island with us.

Un-hugged

Clara Frank

During my daily hike, I find a statue in the canyon, made of grey rectangular, square, rhomboid, and oval rocks. It is shaped like a two-feet-tall man. Or it could be a two-feet-tall robot. It appears fearless, and lonesome as it stands at the edge with his back to the abyss. Below I see parched orange grass and shrubbery, and a dry creek, hardly any rain has fallen this winter season. Railroad tracks cut through the middle, the *Pacific Surfliner* heading for LA just passing through with a slight clatter. Across the canyon, there are luxury mansions, the steep canyon slopes are graced with bright green vegetation, no water shortage there. (Could it be that I live on the wrong side of the tracks?) Above it all, the azure sky, and silky clouds, belong to everyone as the song says. The statue sees none of this, he is facing me, looking at me with his oval "head" slightly askew. As if he were asking a question, a shame, he has no lips to ask. He has no arms to embrace me either. Still, he looks like he needs a hug.

Hugs are hard to come by in this masked world, I tell him as I touch his grainy face with my fingertips. Even if you have arms and lips.

Even when there is no Pandemic.

Thanks for the Memories

Linda Smith

1.

First Dad memory is two-year-old me lying on the wooden floor of our old house on Napa Street. Under the piano, curled close to the legs, I feel vibrations as Dad plays a rowdy Boogie-woogie tune. One slippered foot stomps down while his other foot lands on a pedal. The floor beneath me and the piano canopy above are my cradle; Dad's "HA!" and "Yeah!" and the music he makes with the keys, my lullaby.

2.

Dad loves good food—spareribs and chicken chow mein at his favorite Chinese restaurant, Grandma's blintzes and kreplach, homemade eggplant parmesan, and "Dagwood" style sandwiches piled high with lunch meat, cheese, lettuce, tomatoes, pickles, mayonnaise, mustard and ketchup! On Saturday mornings, sometimes he sends me out to the Jewish Deli on Castor Avenue (where I once fell asleep standing up waiting for my number to be called) and across the street to the bakery. The items always on the list are smoked sable, white fish salad, lox and pickled herring; and from the bakery, pumpernickel bread, poppy seed bagels, salt sticks, Kaiser rolls for sandwiches, and a regular rye bread which for some reason comes from the Jewish deli, not the bakery.

One of the deli's owners (a married couple who each have a tattoo on one arm from concentration camps) puts the rye on a slicer that takes forever to perfectly slice Dad's loaf, also for sandwiches. But it's worth the wait because at home in the kitchen, I am filled with anticipation as the bags of delicacies land on the table before a morning of eating with the family ensues. While I eat my own bagel, it is equally enjoyable to watch and listen as Dad sucks on the head of a fish and picks a bone out from between his teeth or slathers cream cheese on half a bagel, then smothers it with lox. Paying such close attention to everything he does, I wonder if that's how I'll be when I grow up.

3.

Before Dad got his great 1959 powder blue Plymouth, he used to take me and my two older brothers to the silent movies on a Sunday afternoon. We would ride the Number 59 bus, also known as a trackless trolley, the El (short for elevated), and another even older trolley in South Philly. We went the last few blocks by foot, me, the youngest and shortest, hurrying to keep up, trying not to stumble or fall on the cobblestoned streets. Once there, Dad paid something like nickels and dimes and quarters for us to sit and watch and listen to the organ and eat freshly roasted hot peanuts.

The only thing that bothered me about watching Buster Keaton, Charlie Chaplin and Harold Lloyd was that I couldn't read the subtitles. Dad (who was not much of a whisperer) couldn't read them all out loud to me in the small theater where you could hear someone three rows back take a peanut out of a shell. Other than that, those Sundays, including the long bumpy ride home, the relief of getting into my pajamas and going to bed with my stuffed animals, live on as treasured memories.

4.

When *It's a Mad Mad Mad Mad World* came out, Dad had to see it. He worked the night shift and the best time to go was a Saturday matinee. He wouldn't be caught dead going to a Saturday matinee without a carload of kids. By this time, he had that beautiful Plymouth and told me and my brothers to invite a few friends each. We squeezed inside the car and off to the Castor Avenue theater we went.

Once the film started, it was a real contest—should I watch Buddy Hackett and Ethel Merman and the gang onscreen, or Dad, whose laugh is big and loud, mouth wide open, all teeth showing. Sometimes instead of laughing, he'd just say, "WAH!" while his brown eyes with thick dark lashes that look just like mine, twinkled. Dad's "WAH" makes me laugh even now.

5.

No skating backwards, no fancies like jumps or dancing or tricks, just round and round the rink he went while I did my best clinging onto

145

the wall trying to learn balance. Roller skating was another Saturday afternoon activity Dad loved during cold months. Obviously he would not be doing this without a bunch of kids in tow, either. So the boys and I, along with a few friends, crowded into the Plymouth and off to the rink we went. It seems one of the draws for Dad was more organ music which played continuously. It was probably the same old-timey music they played when he first learned. And we could even do the hokey pokey on skates.

6.

Dad also loved to swim and on a hot summer night when he wasn't working the "graveyard shift" he would take us to Max Myers playground where they had a pool, tennis courts and a rec center. He would swim across the pool without ever putting his face in the water. Just moved his head from side to side and kept his arms going while his feet kicked. Or, he did the backstroke, but never the butterfly.

When I was nine and a half and learned how to swim at "Maxie's," the first thing they taught us was to put our faces in the water and turn our heads out for air as slightly as possible. I thought how tiring it must have been for Dad to swim the way he did, but he seemed to enjoy it anyway.

7.

As soon as Dad took early retirement, he and Mom sold the house on Alma Street and moved to Galloway Township in New Jersey, several miles from Atlantic City. Oh how Dad adored the casinos. He always liked games and cards and studied Hoyle's Book of Rules for poker and bridge and other lesser-known games like Klabberjas which of course he taught to us. His two favorite games, poker and keno, were pastimes that lasted the rest of his life. He thought these casinos with the long escalators and plush carpeting were the best thing that ever happened to Atlantic City and he appreciated how they revitalized the place.

When he and Mom came to visit my daughter and I in San Diego, I drove him to El Cajon Boulevard so he could spend an evening in one of the Card Rooms with large plate glass windows looking out onto the street. I worried about him and warned him not to flash his wad of cash

146

around. He laughed and told me not to worry. "I know how to take care of myself."

Sycuan, a casino Dad had read about before coming to visit, offered its patrons free bus rides to and fro. The plan: Dad would have his fun, then catch the last bus going back to the drop-off point where I would pick him up. The reality: he was so caught up talking or whatever, he missed it and I had to drive all the way out there at midnight to get him. It was a weeknight; I had work the next day. It had already been a long week and by time this extra forty-minute-each-way midnight drive came about, I was at the breaking point. Once Dad got into the car, I blurted my feelings out. We were used to communicating that way with each other so even though I was fuming, he let me get it off my chest, then apologized profusely and of course all was forgiven.

8.

Dad had a hat for every occasion. I have a photo of him and my daughter who was two-and-a-half the first time we visited Mom and Dad in New Jersey. He is standing next to her as she sits on a white merry-go-round horse with a blue and green plume. The baseball cap Dad wears says, "I'd Rather be Surfing." To my knowledge, he's never been on a surfboard in his life. In winter he wore a faux fur-lined hat with flaps that fold up, or down to completely cover your ears. Either way, it looks hilarious. When I was little he wore a grey fedora with a black band, especially when we went for dinner at Grandma's house. In summer, it was a Panama hat. He loved hats so much, Mom used to call him Harry-the-Hat.

9.

Dad's health started to decline. He woke up in the middle of the night not feeling well but had rolled over and gone back to sleep. When he saw his doctor a few months later for his yearly physical, the doc said, "it looks like you've had a heart attack." They scheduled him for surgery, Dad had a quadruple bypass and a couple of his arteries were 90-something-percent blocked.

When he told me this on a phone call I said, "how in God's name were you even walking around?"

"Oh, I'm slowing down," is all he said.

10.

He recovered and for years afterwards did all his favorite things, including flying to Las Vegas, driving to Florida, out on a river cruise, frequent trips to AC, wherever poker and gambling was involved.

And then, on a Friday in August 2008, Dad died. He was 82. I couldn't make arrangements to fly back to Philly for the funeral, which Mom insisted had to be early that Sunday morning. I was riddled with guilt and grief and anger.

During the weekend after his death, he "visited" me. Twice. Huge smile with dimples showing, signature 40's style Fedora on his head. At each visit, he nodded as if to say, "I'm okay honey; everything's fine." Dad was in his prime on these visits. Maybe it was before he had children, maybe it was around the time of my birth, who knows? I was overwhelmed by the sight of him so young and happy. So much had happened to us and between us. Filled with emotion but more than anything, grateful to see him again. In the end, it all boiled down to this, "I love you too Daddy. Thank you."

Summer 2020

Nan Valerio

When one has to be in summer quarantine, there are a whole lot worse places to be than at the beach in San Diego. Well, I'm not there, as others are not. It's closed due to the Covid-19 Shutdown.

But, I can see it. The sun is brightening its waves and sparkling its sands. I smell its salty ocean air. Has that air really come from Alaska? Or is it from the tropics of the next state over, Hawaii, 2,500 miles away? Why not? Alaska is that far, too.

The wind moves through the palm fronds, slapping them together and against the tree trunks. This evening, I hope to hear the pandemonium of parrots squawking in those fronds, passing to each other good news about other trees, sagging with sweet ripe fruit that squirrels and rats haven't munched on. I will see those noisy birds take flight, on a secret silent signal, their red and green feathers bright and aggressive.

The sun's warmth on my face, and the ocean breeze mussing my hair, should keep away Covid-19, keep me safe, but might not keep me awake.

Oh, I have my Café Mocha to do that. The hot and slightly bitter liquid beneath the whipped cream now makes me alert.

Slowly sipping my coffee, I sit in my car in the parking lot above the coast, musing on this, my fifth quarantine. I'll make the most of it, if anything can be made of it, and somehow hunker through the isolation as I did in the other quarantines, then for illnesses now controlled by vaccines.

Footprint

Nancy Foley

We stand barefoot in mountain pose, eyes closed
Four corners of feet rooted into the earth. Make
an intention for our practice, she says.
My feet, I'll honor my decades-old feet
Two feet supporting the weight of my body,
26 bones, 33 joints, over a hundred muscles & tendons
like the foundation of a temple, a mobile temple.

My first steps, walking, running, skipping, jumping
footloose, fancy-free, ten toes, standing on my tiptoes
Put your best foot forward, Mom would say
Dad's motto, jump in with both feet. Later his
advice, just get your foot in the door. I think
about being swept off my feet, and after a few years
hearing the patter of little feet, dealing with crow's
feet, now taking a load off my feet.

By age 50, our feet clock 75,000 miles, health experts say
It's no wonder podiatrists treat fallen arches, flat feet
bunions, heel spurs & neuroma. They suggest we take
10,000 steps per day. I want to put my foot down
when my Fitbit shows I'm short for today, but hey, I'm
honoring my feet, so I need to quit dragging my heels.

And for posterity, what impact will my steps have?
Can I help reduce my carbon footprint?
Shake the dust from my feet
Stand on my own two feet, not accept defeat
Or we all may end up six feet under.

Open your eyes, take a deep breath, she says
While connected to the ground, reach your hands
up to the sky. Now bring them to your heart center
and bow your head. Carry your intention with you
throughout the day.

Namaste.

The Eternal Unfolding Moment

Garrett Beaumont

What immediately follows is an edited, word-processed copy of a handwritten stream of consciousness effort in which I tried but failed to live in the moment.

Allow me to write each word I see under eyes unclouded by images concepts memories traumas from the past or worries about the future while I record the following observations as they occur: mind a little dull; eyes a little dry; ears full of sounds near and far; nose itching within its lower left nostril. A cool breeze through a partially open window penetrates the black socks covering my feet crossed at the ankles over the corner of the desk nearest my windows. Thoughts pass by unbidden as I lower my left calf from its desktop perch so I can cross it over my right leg as I sit back on my swivel chair and sense remnants of my lunch within the compound of my midsection. But now a shadow flits briefly across the right-hand margin of the page on which I write, suggesting to me the purple stain which seeped its way through the corners of a stack of three-by-five cards when, several weeks past, I tipped over a glass of wine while sitting in this very chair, that memory suggesting I have now deviated from my goal of writing these pages with eyes unclouded by the past. And now I find a second observation comes to me from the past, albeit the immediate past, in turn triggered by a concept, another unwanted visitor discovered earlier from the past, namely, Jean Paul Sartre's conclusion that the present moment is itself a concept which does not exist since it is gone by the time one's brain registers it.

Postscript:

Although I failed to discover any present moment and therefore failed to live in the moment, I once read and now believe one can sense a present moment outside of reality when one abandons thought. As I grow older I have sensed more and more present moments by thinking as little as I possibly can. However, be warned. Even the sensation of a present moment or living in the moment is destroyed the second you start talking about it.

<><><>

Post Postscript:

More recently I stumbled upon a new device to live in the present moment by renaming it the eternal unfolding moment. With the new name I can collapse all time elapsed from the Big Bang to the unforeseen future and live the remainder of my life with absolute security I live in *that* moment.

Peaceful Times During the Pandemic

Angely Gonzalez

The social distancing pandemic mandates have caused me much discomfort—mainly stress. I like to be active and enjoy people connection and that is extremely limited now-a-days. With the pandemic restrictions and other social issues, it is hard to make peaceful people connection without some type of division or conflict. It is hard to know when people you do not know are smiling, angry, worried, or confused. Their faces are covered—all we see are eyes. A smile is a universal language of peace, acceptance, connection, and friendliness and we can't see it, even if it is there. A smile can diffuse many negative situations. Since I don't know sign language and neither do most people; my index and middle fingers is what I have been using to do the peace sign as a way of letting them know that if I bump into them, it was not my intention and to excuse me. Although I understand the importance of wearing a mask to protect ourselves and others, they are uncomfortable, and they divide us.

When I feel stress, I retreat to what I call my sanctuary—nature. I am at peace when surrounded by nature. There are no loud noises other than birds chirping away so loud that it can drown someone's thoughts, which can be a good thing. A dosage of nature makes me feel great. I love it and am thankful for it. I enjoy watching birds, bees, butterflies, and every little critter as they go about their business in their natural setting—just living without fear or concern. My favorites to watch are the butterflies as they swing so rhythmically up and down as if they were on an air seesaw in slow motion. When I see them, what I hear in my head is Antonio Vivaldi in the *Four Seasons—Spring*. What pleasure to see the peace involved in this. They seem to be flying on an air wave. They go up and down; sometimes they go slow and then speed up again. They seem to be riding on musical notes. Then they make a sudden descent onto the milkweed plant or whatever they are feeding on (that is their rest—a quarter rest or a full rest) where they gather some nectar or maybe lay some eggs.

As beautiful as nature is, many things are deadly for birds and butterflies. Pesticides being some of them, which I am tempted to compare to the coronavirus, since there is a rumor that it is a virus created and delivered to eradicate some of the population and/or for economic purposes. Birds and butterflies also have other predators.

The monarch, for example, lays many eggs all at once. The eggs are smaller than a sugar grain and hardly visible. If harlequins are around, they like to feed on the eggs decreasing the possibility of the eggs ever hatching. If the eggs hatch, they become a caterpillar about the size of one millimeter and can grow to one and a half inches long. But they are still very vulnerable. There is a type of fly called the Tachinid Fly that likes to penetrate their bodies and lay eggs in them. This lets them live but kills them gradually while incubating the flies' eggs. Then there are the spiders. Spiders seem to be harmless, even the small ones; but they destroy the caterpillars with their webs, which tangles them making them defenseless and unable to crawl about to get out to feed.

One afternoon I was watching two butterflies and saw their wings ruffled about. It seemed they were fighting; it was violent—I had never seen them do that before. I got closer to spook them and get them to stop. As I focused my vision, I realized they were mating. "*Wow*," I said to myself, "that resembles people." I videotaped them and posted it on social media and got a few comments and laughs. One of the comments stated they were watching butterfly porn. They may mate like people do and it is obvious they too have their own stressors such as when birds chase each other around, or when hummingbirds are rushing towards each other fighting for territory. I noticed, though, that the critters and birds seem to cope and don't seem to be afraid or concerned. They have all they need and so they are going about their business—just living.

I am thankful for the peacefulness nature offers me. In nature world there is no hostility felt, no hate—there are differences between species, but they are all coping well together in one place. There is no violence, no abuse, nothing unfair going on. Well, there is a little bit of that, but they don't shoot themselves, they don't stab each other. And they don't gang up on one another. They move from one branch or twig to another, and they seem to know how to share their space and accommodate others.

Being surrounded by nature allows me to hear music when there is no music playing. I feel the breeze. I smell the scent of flowers and herbs. I see the mixtures of colors. I wish my sense of smell could be such that I could smell the sweetness of nectar which is what the butterflies and hummingbirds feed on. I know the butterflies can and that is enough for me. What I feel is the joy in watching a world that even with its own conflict and stressors, seems to share peace in their environment. Watching them brings a great feeling of absolute tranquility—serenity to the soul. How great it would be if I could take the peace I feel with nature and transport it to those stressful places where there is anger and strife and turn it into the calmness. The calmness I feel when I see butterflies and birds fly in the air swinging up and down as if they were dancing to another season—A Peaceful Season.

View of Now

Katherine Porter

She arrived at the lookout where
the cliff crumbled
where the sand grains drifted
and the wind blew cold

She stepped away from
her rusted car and watched
from the cliff's collapsing edge
pelicans soared along the brink

She could have left before
all plans were broken by grief
before the virus spun its control
her now would never be the same

She asked herself why
she'd wanted to wade into waves
why she'd wished to sink among fish
drown below shadows of sharks

She knew her old life blew apart
into a life that was already over
apart from the traumas of yesterday
she saw no reason to end life now

She'd leave her baggage behind with
the blustering hope of not knowing
with moments arriving willy-nilly
she'd see where the view of now led

It Once Was Lincoln Memorial

Keith Cervenka

I could tell by the way it felt in my hands. That feel when the ball hits the sweet spot. The baseball flew into the cool October afternoon sky, going, going, gone—over the gravel path. "Home Run!" I yelled, then started my round-tripper trot.

"That ball hit the edge of the path," Paul Smith shouted from centerfield. "That's not a homer!"

Paul was one of a family of ten kids, eight boys and two girls. We always went to their house first when looking for players.

I took off running while Paul dashed into the woods, chasing my "oh-so-close-to-a-home run" ball. As I rounded second, I glanced over my shoulder and saw him coming out of the trees, making his throw to third base where Steve stood ready to make the catch and tag. A teammate yelled, "My God, Cervenka, unhitch that U-Haul."

I knew Paul's arm wasn't that good but I also knew Steve was the best ballplayer in the neighborhood. That's why we nicknamed him Star. He went on to play college ball at Bradley University and now sells auto and homeowners' insurance. My legs churned and arms pumped as I streaked for third.

Star reached for the ball as I started my slide onto the rock-hard dirt. We all hated to slide because it usually left a painful strawberry. But sometimes we just had to. My foot hit the square piece of cardboard as Star's glove hit my leg. "Safe!"

"You're out!" Star cried. "My glove gotcha before your foot hit the base. You're out."

"Safe!" I screamed again as if yelling louder made it so. I stood, then dragged the piece of cardboard back into position with my toe. The strawberry on my thigh already began to hurt.

Paul came charging in from center field shouting, "You're out, you're out," even though he was too far away to see anything. Tim, the youngest of the Smiths, who we called Squirt, ran in from left field, "You're out Keith, I could see it clear."

"Aw, get out of here, Squirt," I said. "You can't see over the grass."

Jim Smith scrambled to third from his catcher's position yelling, "You're out, Cervenka."

Under the hedge-apple tree, near our stolen wire-gate-turned-backstop, stood John Smith. "Tie goes to the runner," he shouted. Boober and Grease, the Bobbitt brothers, charged across the field hollering, "Safe. He was safe." Boober's now a Rod Stewart impersonator and makes more money than all of us.

The rhubarb was on. Twelve biased umpires yelling, pointing, and spitting.

I turned sixteen that summer and was two months into my junior year at Richwoods High School. The guys who started their senior year found cooler things to do than play baseball with us. A couple of guys who graduated the year before had gotten their draft cards. Pat Smith joined the Army and was stationed in Germany. Greg joined the Navy to avoid his boots on the ground in Vietnam. It was the summer of Woodstock, even though from my small patch of the world in Peoria, Illinois I wasn't sure what or where that was.

The Mets played the Orioles in the World Series that October, which meant we would soon be putting our bats and gloves away and bringing out our footballs and helmets. That was the last time I played baseball with my friends at the field we built as kids and named Lincoln Memorial. Some of the younger guys played the following summer, but I was a senior by then with cooler things to do.

I'm not as cool now as I was fifty years ago. Hopefully, I'm cooler today than I will be twenty years from now. I imagine someday being pushed down a Rosewood Care Center corridor in a wheelchair by a young nurse. She makes a wide turn at the exact spot where the Lincoln Memorial second base used to be. Now I'm bookin' for third. I glance over my shoulder to see if the centerfielder's making his throw. I turn back and there's Star straddling third base, waiting to make the catch and tag. As I get closer, I see it's actually a nurse, probably one of the Smith's grandchildren, hovering over the piece of cardboard. She wears a disturbing smile while clutching a silver bedpan.

I don't think I'll be sliding this time.

A Window's View of the World

Hiedi Woods

I've been hanging here for over a hundred years. A skilled craftsman carefully measured the square, nailed in the outer frame, fitted the screen, added two thick, heavy panes of crystal-clear glass. As he rigged the pulleys and ropes, I came alive. He tested me, closing and opening, opening and closing. I worked. Then he gently hammered on the casing, my crowning glory that took me from functional window to work of art. Made of dark walnut with decorative millwork circles in the corners and carved sides, my casing made me a classic example of Queen Anne Victorian architecture. There are eight other windows on the second floor. No, I'm not one of the triplets that grace the elegant turret, and no, I don't have stained glass like my downstairs cousin. However, I do have a special place in the history of the house.

I remember the day the young couple moved in with their baby daughter. They bought the entire house—all three floors—but kept the second and third floors for themselves. Another young family rented the first floor. A new dad, The Boss, loved to hold the baby on his hip and let her look out of me into the big wide world. Her fat little hands banged on my glass, but I didn't mind. Her giggles made me smile, and she was so cute in her pink frilly dress and blonde curls.

It might be difficult to imagine that a window would have much of a story to tell. However, my position at the front corner of the second floor living room made me important in the family of windows. Could the little bathroom window on the side of the house oversee the kids running around the front yard? Could the pretty kitchen window in the back with the bright yellow curtains see the rain reflected in the streetlight across the way and give a weather update? The daily comings and goings might have been boring to some but not to me. So much activity—the postman, the milkman, the back-and-forth to work and school. Everyone leaving for a day at the beach, laughing and excited, and then back home in the evening tired and cranky. The Boss's Wife, Lady Boss, lovingly took care of me, polishing my wood frame, cleaning my glass. She always left me spotless. Through the years, many cats smeared against me on my sill watching with me: Lady, Henry, Lucy,

160

Gingko, Tigger, Venus, Chloe, and lots of kittens. On hot summer days, a cat would sprawl out on my sill, fur crushed against the screen to catch a breeze. The silky coat felt warm and comforting.

Some days were more exciting than others. I witnessed the next four babies arrive home in the Buick. I watched them, as children, ride bikes and sleds and, later, as teens, how to back the car out of the long driveway. With the house located near the bottom of the hill, I could see almost to the top of the hill and all the way down, and so could anyone using me to look outside. The teenagers loved to watch for their friends' cars coming to pick them up for parties and beach trips. I saw them in party dresses and tuxes, in sports uniforms, in caps and gowns, then drive away by themselves to be gone for a long time and thankfully return.

Every season had its special moments. In spring, The Boss worked hard on the front garden, and through his hands came a riot of color: rhododendron, forsythia, pansies, dahlias, lilac. Summer brought big, booming thunderstorms, and children home all the time, playing outside until the fireflies came out. In the fall, the wind blew the leaves and school started again with new shoes and first-day outfits. Winter was my favorite season. With my position at a front corner, I had a special neighbor for several weeks every year, the Christmas tree. I loved displaying the bright colorful lights to the world outside. On snowy nights, the kids would use me every few minutes to check the snowfall rate in the streetlamp glow across the way. A heavy snow often meant no school the next day, and then the day would be spent watching the kids happily sled down our hill.

Over the years the children grew and moved to their own houses, but they still visited. Once, there was a big party in the backyard. The activity started early in the morning as workers carried in chairs, tables, and trays filled with food. For the first time, I wished I was in the back of the house. I missed the party, but I got to see guests dressed in dark suits and fancy dresses, their arms laden with brightly colored presents. Then the bride and groom arrived amidst cheers and toasts. I was glad I was in the front because that party lasted long into the night, way past bedtime for the house.

Eventually babies began arriving again. The Boss was now a grandpa, and he was home a lot. He stopped leaving for work and became the babysitter. My sill was the perfect height for the toddlers to rest their hands on me and look out or pet the kitties sleeping on me.

161

When the babies went home it was different. Grandpa liked the quiet and took long naps on the couch near me.

The Boss always dressed nicely even if only to go grocery shopping. He was what could be called old school: button down shirt, dress pants, loafers, and the always-present fedora. One day he dressed and went shopping early. Lady Boss was still working at the time and gone all day. When she got back, The Boss was still not home. Their youngest by this time had moved to the city, however, she arrived for a visit and to do laundry. I could tell Lady Boss was worried because she was chain-smoking. I could smell it all the way from the back porch.

This made me anxious too. The Boss never stayed out for long. I welcomed a fellow watcher to share my view of the street as the daughter perched on the couch arm next to me to hold vigil. I could feel her tension as she willed the sight of her dad's car to appear on our hill. Venus, the fat tabby, was our only companion. She watched, too, a nervous meow now and then. She was most concerned that the boss wouldn't be home to feed her. She had him wrapped around her little paw. Around dinner time, Venus always came into the living room where The Boss was watching the news and meowed sadly at him. She usually turned her nose up at the Friskies, and he had to get her ham from the fridge.

After several hours, a police car came down the hill and turned into the driveway. The daughter shouted the news, and she and her mother ran to the back of the house where the entry was. What was happening? Where was the Boss?

A serious-looking state trooper came into the living room with the family. The trooper found him driving on the highway shoulder about fifteen miles out, heading away from home. The Boss couldn't explain what happened, except he suddenly didn't know where he was.

After that, we spent even more time together. He didn't drive anymore and would sit near me to read and nap, both of us in a comfortable silence. We aged together. My ropes started fraying, my wood fading, my glass just a little scratched, spotted with dust.

One day the furniture changed, and the Boss and Lady Boss moved into the first-floor apartment. The stairs are difficult for them, so I don't see them much. For a time, I ached for the old days, my bosses—my friends—the comings and goings, the happy children and rambunctious grandchildren, the sparkling Christmas tree, the sleepy cats.

I was excited when a young couple rented the second floor. There was so much activity—moving in, excited chatter, decorating, having friends over to show off their home. I looked forward to getting to know my new family. However, they are not here very often. And when they are, they always talk about work or are preoccupied with their many screens, too busy to take notice of me. They mostly keep the curtains closed.

Messengers

Elliott Linwood

Part One: Vignette

That humid summer morning, my brother and I painstakingly working our way into a blackberry thicket to reach the ripest fruit. It's very still. Until it isn't. Stepping on a ground nest of angry wasps, all hell dislodged itself.

While the limbic part of our brains cascaded into a fight or flight response, the mind encountered a dilemma. Options in a millisecond: faced with being stung or being shredded by the maze of enormous thorns, rational consciousness kicked in to slow things down. Zombies, playing dead to stay alive, we slowly backed our asses out of the briars.

What doesn't kill you makes you stronger—I was stung the least and screamed the most. Otherwise, it causes shock—my brother remains anaphylactic to this day.

Part Two: Odes and Manifestos

Throat clearing cue, as if to sing: By the time I reached San Francisco during the AIDS crisis around 1983, parades on the East Coast proclaimed with industrial militancy that Silence = Death. Whereas, on the left coast, buoyed, perhaps, by more mascara, the abridged slogan affirmed that Action = Life.

Years of epithets and epitaphs followed, as the specter of acres of kitsch on casket-sized quilts lay festooned on the National Mall in Washington, DC, the closest many had to funerals.

My day job, then, in electronic publishing, involved turning laundry lists into holograms. I designed scientific catalogs of body tissues, viral reagents, lab kits and other materials researchers might wish to order. I'd reconfigure databases to generate indices cross-referencing different sections of these books, with bleed tabs that could be easily thumbed through by their users. That the design lingo, deployed toward biological subject matter carried an uncanny eeriness, still seems strange, particularly now.

Leslie Jamison, in *The Recovering: Intoxication and Its Aftermath,* notes that the word *cliché* mimics the sound of metal plates in a printing press. Having commonly used phrases on hand instead of resetting individual letters each time, was about utility and expediency.

Since Covid-19 isn't my first viral rodeo, I hear machinations from those days still
. . . cliché, cliché, cliché.

Part Three: Koans and Acronyms

My interest in writing involves stewardship and revisionism, in appraising the kinds of artwork I have done, with a nuanced sense of history. Articulation, however, is the trick.

In Buddhism, speech—deemed an ethical practice—asks whether what I'm saying is honest, heartfelt, useful, or appropriate? Whereas, in performance art, language froths around seduction, in order to instruct. The major difference being that if someone or something appears intoxicating from across the room, though that might be successful art, the Buddhist koan beseeches us to *TURN AROUND AND RUN!*

My favorite acronyms, Why Am I Talking? (WAIT), and its refrain, Why Am I Still Talking? (WAIST) are cues to wrap things up. If my first vignette depicted a kind of temporalization of space between the brain and the mind's momentum, then I'd like to diagram hiccups in the spatialization of time through one last example.

Imagine roaring down the freeway, listening to music from two centuries ago, composed when the artist was deaf, never intended to be performed. Our current technological global nervous system of social media and geolocation—besides surveilling and projecting information—pries open, instantaneously, new ways for us to witness and value each other more widely and profoundly. Who lives to tell the tale? Mortality = Mobilization.

Chinese Knots

Chi Ping Hu

Paleolithic age, Chinese knots emerged
Rulers ruled
events recorded
before written characters existed
history and civilization traced

Qing Dynasty, popularized
affordable to any social status or budget
bring commoners happiness
lucky accessories, friends' gifts, home decorations

Nowadays, giftshops in Chinatown
dazzle under afternoon sunshine
so many choices on Amazon
valentine token, car pendant, new year present,
budget-friendly feasts for the eyes

Countless styles fit for any occasion
each with a distinct meaning

Named after its pattern or symbolic thoughts
Homophonic words borrowed to express blessings
convey deep emotion
but all connotate "I wish everything goes well!"

Top to bottom
silk cord weaved into a loop
ends tasseled, symmetrical in shape
pottery, glass, jade, and wood as the material

Blue noble orchid
one of four gentlemen flowers
in traditional Chinese painting
hand-painted on both sides
the hexagonal pottery vase
gifted by Teacher Chen
for teaching her son

Two fishes hold a glass ball
hung in houses during the new year
bestow good luck
four words in the center form a phrase
year after year an abundant fall harvest

A six-word phrase is carved into
ring-shaped white nephrite knots
to heal and guide,
raw jade is worthless until it is polished
one cannot have success without trials
heirlooms passed for generations
in it, I see my parents' faces

A little barefoot carved on redwood
Big toe bent—a tiny spider on top
fits perfectly in my left palm
whenever I muse or read
I fondle it for hours, not wanting to put it down
the more I play, the smoother the surface
In Chinese, spider and fulfillment are homophonic
Lao-Zi's philosophic proverb:
"Happiness lies in contentment"

Chinese knots crystallize
through different art forms
aim for the highest goals:
truth, perfection, and beauty for all

The Tiger Ladies:
A Memoir of Friendship and Fantasy

Sandra Sinrud

The summer I was nine, our small Southern California town enjoyed a post-war housing boom and entire neighborhoods seemed to appear overnight. A family that moved in next door to us had a girl my age, and we quickly became forever friends. We were enamored with heroic dramas on television and inspired by a particular episode of a friendship between an American Indian and a rancher's son, we pricked our thumbs and held them tight together to become blood sisters. Very little blood was actually involved, but our thumbs throbbed anyway, and we felt our bond was complete.

As blood sisters, we became heroes of our own favorite fantasy. We roamed the smooth new sidewalks riding imaginary horses as . . . Tiger Ladies! Why tigers? Only my nine-year-old self knows. Oblivious to mixed metaphors, our fantasy costumes consisted of Lone Ranger masks and black bodysuits emblazoned with orange stripes.

Thus empowered, we traversed the neighborhood keeping a watchful eye on little children at play and checking backyards for suspicious activity. Is that a thief sneaking around in Mrs. Johnson's yard? No, it's just Mr. Johnson watering his azaleas. Oh-oh, that kid on the playground looks lost. Never mind, there's his mother. We were confident we could handle any crisis, real or imagined, although the imagined ones were more frequent—an attempted kidnapping perhaps, armed robbery, or—and would behave heroically under pressure.

Any passersby saw two ordinary girls wearing blue jeans and T-shirts, never suspecting they were passing Tiger Ladies in full regalia riding two prancing, snorting horses. At noontime, we went to our respective homes to rest our steeds and have lunch. Mom made me grilled cheese sandwiches and tomato soup, my favorite lunch, followed by just-out-of-the-oven chocolate fudge brownies. Once fortified, I rejoined my friend and we returned to duty overseeing the neighborhood. "Be back in time for dinner, honey," Mom would say. She called me "honey" because not even she knew my secret identity.

Being nine was perfect—beyond childish youth, confident of my abilities, and relatively untouched by adult expectations. It helped that I had two older sisters and as the "baby" of the family, I got a free pass on most chores. This baby, however, didn't consider herself a baby. She believed herself to be a fully capable person, of whom greater things should be expected.

I had two sisters, and as a Tiger Lady, I took it hard that my twelve-year-old sister was frivolous enough to adorn her room with organdy curtains and, possibly worse, silly enough to be mesmerized by the televised coronation of Queen Elizabeth II. But at least she talked to me occasionally. My fourteen-year-old sister and I barely had a speaking relationship, unless you count the times she yelled at me to get out of her room.

One winter evening, while using our treadle-operated Singer sewing machine, my sister—the one who talked to me sometimes—ran the needle through the nail of her index finger. She screamed, and our mom ran to her and extricated the finger, needle still attached, from the apparatus.

My father telephoned the family doctor and we all piled into our olive green '47 Chevy sedan to rush to his office. It was after hours, but in those days the family doctor would open his office at night to see a patient. My sister sat in the back with her hand in a copper-bottomed Revere Ware saucepan sloshing with water and ice cubes. I was proud of her—she was pretty stoic for a non-Tiger Lady.

The streets were wet and shiny from recent rains. Nearing the doctor's office, an ambulance siren caused our dad to divert down a residential street. His avoidance tactic didn't work. Siren screaming, red lights piercing the darkness, the ambulance was headed straight for us. The street was too narrow to avoid a collision. We're goners, I thought, a tragedy to be told on the evening television news and in the morning newspaper. By the time our dad tucked the car safely into a driveway, I was halfway out the door, preparing to roll free and save myself. As the ambulance slid harmlessly by, I sheepishly closed the door and joined in the relief and laughter of the others. My laughter masked my shame, and my Tiger Lady persona deflated a little.

At the doctor's, our near-death experience was forgotten by everyone but me as my sister was hustled into the office. How could I have considered abandoning my family? I should've stayed and accepted my fate with the others. When my sister emerged from the office with a bandaged finger, we all piled back into the car and were home before bedtime. The bandage came off a few days later, and all she had was a little dimple in her fingernail.

The school year came and went, and summer rolled around again. One day, while helping my dad weed and water in the backyard, our neighbor's wooden storage shed was suddenly swathed in thick black smoke billowing from gaps in the sides. No sooner had we noticed it, with a WOOSH the smoke blossomed into flame. Glass shattered and fire shot out of the broken windows, accompanied by loud thuds and bumps. Was someone inside, trying to escape and unable to find the door? My inner Tiger Lady told me I could—should, even—jump the fence and smash down the door, yet I remained frozen with fear.

As my dad directed the water hose at the shed, he yelled for me to call the fire department. Relieved for an excuse to run away with legitimate purpose, I dialed "0" for operator on our rotary telephone. It seemed to take forever for the dial to return to its starting position and for the operator to answer. She sent the fire department, and the blaze was quickly extinguished. The thuds and bumps, we learned, were exploding paint cans. No one was injured, and amazingly, no one noticed my cowardice. Except me.

I knew my father thought I was only a child and forgave what I considered to be my failure to help. Not me. I was ten years old now and over four feet tall—practically a grown-up.

Before the school year started again, my friend-in-fantasy moved away when her father was stationed abroad. Blood sisters we may have been, but the bond didn't extend all the way to Guam. The Tiger Lady faded from my life—a necessary loss in the process of growing up, but a loss nonetheless.

Many decades have passed, and I know my reactions to those events were appropriate for my age, but I didn't know that then. My fantasy-self urged my real-life self to act heroically in spite of the fact that there was an actual adult present to handle the situation. Later, with daughters of my own, I did, in fact, meet and conquer real-life crises. Perhaps it was my inner Tiger Lady rising to the occasion. Who knows? What I do know is that I'm grateful to have known her—to have been her—for that brief period of time.

Children around the world suffered then, and suffer now, real-life terrors and crises far beyond the darkest imaginings of my nine-year-old self. No longer insulated in bucolic neighborhoods, 24-hour news and social media bring the terrors home—gun violence, social injustice, climate change, and more. It gives me hope that many young activists have emerged to address these challenges and to demand change. Perhaps the little children will lead us after all.

In Defense of Rhyme

Garrett Beaumont

Let us please ourselves with that tonic called rhyme
which when we employ it works most of the time
I don't mean by that we must shout with delight
and yet if we did it would be quite all right
For rhyme's like a balm; it smooths and it steadies
and turns crashing waves into mild-mannered eddies
Many poets today look at rhyme as a blight
It's the forcing of word choice that makes them uptight
If they'd open their hearts and look back at Poe
they might see that rhyme was a good way to go
Just reread *The Raven* or *Annabelle Lee*
Poe rhymed all the time yet with words was quite free
His rhymes oft drew pictures, mine generally do not
But even my rhymes feature themes or a plot
And if my word choices fall short of sublime
I'll shoulder the blame, please spare glorious rhyme

The Purpose of a Black Skirt

Hiedi Woods

How many black skirts do I actually need? I often wonder while flipping through the racks of TJ Maxx, Nordstrom Rack, J Jill or even Target (pronounce it French-like, please—*Tar-jey*). There is no easy answer because there are too many variations—length, fabric, plain or design. I love to shop, especially for bargains. I can have more than I need because I get them at good prices. And then there is the fact that well, I look good in a lot of different styles. Don't even get me started on skirts for different seasons. I don't care that I live in Southern California; we have seasons I tell you. Putting on a certain piece of clothing can change your mood, your outlook, your personality—even for only a day.

My favorite black skirt for when I need a bit more than business casual is from Target. It is simple polyester, straight cut, just past the knee, side slit, all-season weight, machine wash, air dry, no iron. Perfection in a few yards of fabric. I pair it with a proper blouse and blazer, pumps, and usually my pearls because I am ladylike and business-like. It's the first thing I pack on every business trip, which usually means the New York City office. This basic skirt makes me feel accomplished, confident, and professional, especially in New York where most women look like they just stepped out of a fabulous boutique on an unlimited budget.

New York City—a shopping mecca. I love visiting that office. Not only do I get to see my colleagues and occasionally family and friends from my home state of Connecticut, it's also a mommy break. No dashing around the house, begging my son to eat his breakfast, remembering to feed the cat. Waking up in my comfy, quiet Midtown hotel room, my only cares to shower, dress, and do makeup before I stroll down 6th Avenue for the short walk to the office, wearing that Target skirt.

After work, the city is my playground. I am often on my own as colleagues head off on their hellish commutes. All I need to do is wander around, soak in the atmosphere, eat a nice dinner, and do a little shopping maybe. I don't have to rush home for orthodontist appointments, karate lesson drop-off, or even to exercise with all the city walking. The famed 5th Avenue is the perfect destination. H&M alone is three floors! One of my favorite finds—a black skirt, knee length, high paper bag waist with lots of soft folds, an unexpected brown belt—so cute, flirty, feminine. Just what you need on a mommy break.

Not all my black skirts are solid color. One of my favorite places to shop was TJ Maxx before they got fancy and started selling a lot of designer wear. I can't make myself spend $75 on a dress from a discount place. That is not the point, TJ Maxx buyers! We are looking for bargains and one-of-a-kind finds! Browsing pretty clothes, finding a bargain is for me like a shot of happiness.

Some people don't like to shop in discount stores. It's an upper-body workout, balancing a pile of clothes on one arm while your other hand inspects the clothes like a detective. Look at that three-mile-long row, crammed with hangers. It's not really three miles, but it feels like it after you spend fifteen minutes moving each hanger down the line, the metal hook scraping the bar, lulling you into a trance. It is kind of meditative now that I think about it.

Scrape, brown skirt, scrape, red flower skirt, scrape, blue skirt, scrape, white shirt, how did that get in here, scrape, black skirt, scrape. WAIT. What was that?

I can tell just by looking that it is mine. It's beautiful. I touch the fabric—soft linen. I assess the length—past the knee. I peek inside—lined—a sign of quality. My eyes travel over it, and I fall in love. Black, yes, but with a swirling pattern of blue flowers, embroidered, possibly hand stitched. I hold my breath as I flip over the price tag—$12. Life is good.

There are other black skirts in my closet—denim, faux suède, velvet—I was wearing the velvet one when I met Al Pacino. I think there are a few more and that is ok. They each serve a purpose—confidence boosting, flirtatious, to brighten my day, or evoke a fond memory. I'm not sure what one I need today, but I think there's a sale at J Jill.

Fashion Statements

Bil Fuhrer

Parenting: A Game with no rules, taught to us by our children

Fashion awareness blossoms when you are six, when you're a girl. When our daughter, Cindy, returned from her first day in kindergarten, she announced that the kids were great, the teacher was boring, and she desperately needed to upgrade her image by piercing her ears and purchasing designer jeans. Public school had made her a fashion-conscious, independent thinking woman in one day. Upon further investigation, I discovered the jeans in question cost eighty-five dollars and would fit her for approximately three weeks at the rate she was growing. I also learned that Ms. Boring was a twenty-nine-year-old beauty queen with black hair that flowed to the middle of her back, drove a Porsche convertible, and was setting all-time attendance records at parent-teacher meetings. Patti was swift to handle Cindy's piercing request.

"Go ask your father." Cindy translated it thus:

"Mommy says it's okay to pierce my ears if it's okay with you."

She had discovered a universal truth: when negotiating with parents on tough issues like this, keep them separated. United they stand, divided they relent. So, there she was, the child who cries just thinking about getting a flu shot, begging me to let her get her ears punctured. Fashion is apparently a force more powerful than pain, kind of like stilettos. I explained why the piercing would not proceed as clearly as I could.

"Cindy, I'm not going to let some tattooed, spike-haired, body-pierced, teenage goth punker drive rivets through your ears with a contaminated staple gun. You will get an infection, lose an ear, or worse. You're six. Let's wait 'til you're eighteen."

But fashion is a force not easily subdued. Soon after my pronouncement, I met Bruce, a graphics designer from Lucas Films in Hollywood. He had a pet llama named Cleopatra. Bruce came to my company to demonstrate how he and his design team had used our computers to create aircraft fight scenes including one of the most successful computer simulation films ever, *Star Wars*. Bruce had braided dreadlocks, wore a baby blue tank top, sheer puffy pink pants, and gold slippers. He looked much like a genie just out of the bottle as he sat quietly in the corner waiting to be introduced. Sheer means very thin or transparent and that definition came alive when Bruce stood up to speak. He wore no underwear under those sheer puffy pantaloons. His animated style added to the audience's embarrassment as he pranced back and forth between the computer screen and his storyboard. He was passionate about his presentation and apparently unaware of this ancillary exhibition. It was some minutes before I realized that in addition to his graphic display, he had five hoops hanging from each ear. How could I have missed those? Then, I noticed he had also pierced his tongue and a gold stud was flashing and flapping in there as he lectured. It was quite a sight: Bruce sashaying back and forth across the room like a ballerina, hoops swaying, tongue stud flashing and old Obi Wan Kenobi down there, swinging back and forth in plain sight. Cindy's request to pierce her ears suddenly seemed benign, even reasonable by comparison.

We finally gave in to her piercing pleas. Our home was harmonious once again until I learned that one set of ear holes is not sufficient fashion. After a few months, a second set appeared. I pretended not to notice, choosing harmony over conflict.

"Have you noticed Cindy's ears lately?" asked Patti.

"No," I lied, choosing harmony over truth.

Ear embellishment continued. I correctly guessed it would stop at five, reasoning that Bruce, the Hollywood flasher and trendsetter, had established that fashion limit.

It wasn't until years later when Cindy was eighteen that the next two impalements appeared: one navel, one nose.

"How do you like them Dad? They're a birthday present to myself."

The diamond in the navel made me tremble as I thought about what Craftsman tool might have been necessary to install it and the thing in her nose looked more like an infected zit than a ruby. I wondered what she would do when she gets a runny nose. I decided to swallow my zit thought.

"Wow," I choked. "Latest in fashion, I assume."

"His name is Neil, Dad. He's just a friend. I want you to meet him but please don't freak out when you see how he dresses. He's a little different but very nice and really smart. He's on the debate team."

My mind flashed back to Bruce, only this time he was coming to our house, probably driving a purple van with carpeting on the ceiling and a cocktail table and quick-release convertible couch in the back.

Neil wore black leather everything, butch-waxed, spiked hair, silver chains hanging from the pockets and bracelets with half-inch spikes on his wrists. His right eyebrow was pierced with a silver ring and a matching one was stuck through his lip. Connecting the two rings was a silver chain that dangled on his cheek. When he spoke, the chain bobbed in random and distracting ways, and a silver stud punctured through his tongue became visible. I shuddered to think about the stud's purpose. The motion of the chain and the reflective flashes from his mouth were hypnotic. As he told me about his band and building a soundproof studio in his parent's garage, I wondered if he was aware that his undulating chain was a fine example of Chaos Theory. I wondered if there were any words or phrases that could set the chain into harmonic motion. I wanted him to say Zimbabwe, Botswana and Okavango Delta. I wanted him to say Obi Wan Kenobi and C3PO.

Later, Cindy said, "Neil thinks you're really cool, Dad. He said you're a great listener . . . for a parent."

She stood there smiling with her ten earrings, nose stud and navel diamond all glistening in the afternoon light. Nice fashion statement, I thought. Not too plain, not too fancy: no lip ring, no chain, no tongue stud, no genie pants. Just my lovely eighteen-year-old daughter making a subtle fashion statement.

Hands

Chi Ping Hu

The first time we meet, my eyes discover
your big hands seem larger than average.
Is your palm wider, or fingers longer?
You turn the steering wheel with only one
hand making swift turns on the rocky road
perfect for playing a grand piano
ideal for holding a basketball
one hand blocks while the other takes a shot.
Your hands were trained by a kung fu master
put through countless practice and tender care
medicine placed on bruises & injuries
martial arts' rules—force as the last resort
years without piano or basketball
with hands held through these memorable years.

Sisterhood

Sandra Sinrud

Sisterhood is not a simple brew. It is a complex emotional stew with many richly nourishing ingredients—sweet childhood memories, savory support, tender thoughtfulness. But no sisterhood is complete without conflict—bitter disagreements, unpalatable selfishness, and sour disappointments are added to the pot. When such toxic ingredients are allowed to increase, they taint the pot, and the stew becomes cloudy and muddled. Love and affection sink out of sight. As the pot burbles, the ingredients blend, the savory and the unsavory; but then with care and replenishment, the buoyant, life-affirming morsels increase and rise to the top within easy reach.

Obligation and responsibility are part of the process, but properly maintained, all who partake are nurtured and satisfied.

This sisterly concoction enriches our lives. Sometimes one sister or another has greater need of nourishment, but over time each takes, and each contributes. The brew, after all, is not self-sustaining—it needs to be tended mindfully. One must be watchful. Like that of Macbeth's witches, our brew requires more than a little "toil and trouble." But unlike their steaming cauldron, our humble pot has no aspirations to bring forth a "hellbroth." With a little luck and a lot of effort, it will instead produce a never-ending supply of sisterly sustenance.

Love Note After WCW

Lloyd Hill

I ate a loquat from those
you chose a few days ago
when they were yellow.

They're in the icebox
for us this afternoon.

They're bronzed now
overripe but sweeter
more to my taste.

Memories

Georganna Holmes

How quickly the years roll on
like elm, oak leaves on the fly
when hurly-burly autumn winds
strew them across the sky.

Where do they go, stacked
with moments of our bliss:
first cry of the newborn babe?
that handsome Romeo's first kiss?

My advice: take pen in hand,
record them all while you are young.
Because you won't remember them,
I swear, when you are ninety-one.

Author Biographies
and Index

ShuJen Walker Askew
(71)
ShuJen writes in a variety of genres. Her work is published in literary magazines at Mesa College, Grossmont College, San Diego Writers & Editors Guild, and San Diego Writers Ink. Her writing is recognized in the Top 10 of the San Diego Decameron Project. ShuJen loves writing and hopes that one day her children will read her work.

◇◇◇

Norma Kipp Avendano
(141)
Norma grew up in Georgia, married, and became a mother and home-maker in two happy marriages. She is twice a widow. A successful teacher for twenty years, she is also a photographer, artist, author, world traveler, collector and teacher of Mexican folk art and has many, many friends.

◇◇◇

Garrett Beaumont
(152, 172)
Garrett, from the East Bay town of Lafayette, is a graduate of UC Berkeley and UCLA Law School when the world was young. He published a law book near the end of his legal career, joined Workshop as a retired lawyer, and now as a retiree is writing a lengthy biography of Rita Hayworth, which resides in his computer.

◇◇◇

Walt Besecker
(98)
Walt worked most of his adult life in a variety of public service positions in the Washington, DC area before moving with his wife Susan, of 53 years, to SD in 2019. He dreams of writing and only recently began to make that dream a reality.

Tim Calaway
(6, 57, 109)
Tim is a writer living in San Diego. He writes poems, short stories, and even shorter stories, as well as the occasional novel.

◇◇◇

Keith Cervenka
(17, 110, 158)
Keith is from Peoria, Illinois. He lives in Southern California and is a graduate of Western Illinois University. Now retired, he worked eighteen years in the construction business before working for twenty years as a Certified Financial Planner. Currently, he is writing a historical novel, which is loosely based on his great-grandparents' lives.

◇◇◇

Bjorn Endresen
(58)
Born in Norway in 1950, Bjorn is the father of two daughters, and grandfather to five. After four years in the Navy, he went into sales and consulting, before tiring of that at age 45. After traveling and sailing around the world for five years, during which he met his wife, Pauline, he now lives in San Diego since 2002. He is new to poetry.

◇◇◇

Laura Fitch
(48)
Laura Fitch has been drawing and writing, since her teens while growing up in Tijuana, and in San Diego where she still resides. She learned English by discovering a Mark Twain story excerpt in a 5th grade book, and Edgar Alan Poe, Stephen King, and Gabriel Garcia Marquez inspired her teen reading, so she hopes the stories she writes reflect that.

◇◇◇

Nancy Foley
(46, 55, 97, 150)
Nancy's writing appears in the *San Diego Poetry Annual, California Quarterly Journal, A Year in Ink, S. D. Union Tribune, Reader, Summation,* and four anthologies. Winner of the 2021 Catholic Literary Arts Poetry Contest, Nancy has been a member of the Workshop

since 2007. Her writing is enriched by stories of her nine grand-children.

◇◇◇

Clara Frank
(78, 143)
Clara, born in Budapest, Hungary, is a retired Hospital Epidemiologist, a Red Cross volunteer, and a proud grandmother of two grandsons. Her short stories and essays are found in literary magazines, and she is working on a novel in which most of the action takes place in Hungary under German and Russian occupation.

◇◇◇

Bil Fuhrer
(15, 175)
Bil, originally from central Pennsylvania, holds an Electrical Engineering degree from Penn State. He moved to California to thaw out. Married to his college sweetheart, they have two daughters and two grandkids. He loves traveling but is temporarily staying safe, staying healthy, staying home and writing. He loves creating short humorous pieces and sometimes he succeeds.

◇◇◇

Michele Garb
(133)
Michele is published on cloth and is a bestselling author in her own mind. Others disagree. She spends her time trying to teach her four-legged serial killer the error of her ways. When not playing Disney movies for her pet, you can find her breathing and typing—her dog hunting nearby.

◇◇◇

Angely Gonzalez
(121, 154)
Born in the Dominican Republic, Angely grew up in Brooklyn, New York, then moved to San Diego, making it her home since 1981. She holds a Bachelor's degree from San Diego State University and a Master's degree from National University. Her participation in SDCCE Writer's Workshops continues since 2010.

◇◇◇

Nadia Harris
(65)
A resident of San Diego since retiring from American University where she taught French Studies, Nadia, together with her husband, migrates to Maine most summers. Through the San Diego College of Continuing Education Writer's Workshop, she explores the joys of writing fiction, creative nonfiction, and memoir.

◇◇◇

Janis Heppell
(11)
Janis, a native San Diegan, enjoyed a career in Marketing before retiring in 2014. She began writing short stories as a personal challenge and discovered a new passion. Her personal essays and a selection of her short stories can be found on her blog:
RetirementallyChallenged.com.

◇◇◇

Lloyd Hill
(21, 102, 140, 180)
Lloyd, SDSU alum, longtime Ocean Beach poet. Spoken word to lyric, cafes to classrooms to Zooms. Winner of *Musings* Poetry Prize and Pier Poets facilitator. His accomplished poetry is found in *San Diego Poetry Annual, City Beat, Serving House Journal, The Stories Start Here, Amazing Writers,* and elsewhere.

◇◇◇

Georganna Holmes
(22, 54, 90, 181)
Georganna is the author of many chapbooks of poetry. Since retiring from the San Diego Public Library system, she still loves books so much that she even worked as a library volunteer. Now living in North County, she writes, reads, and does crossword puzzles. Another chapbook may be forthcoming soon.

◇◇◇

Chi Ping Hu
(10, 114, 166, 178)

Chi Ping Hu, a Chinese-born American and San Diego resident for over 41 years, joined the SDCCE Writer's Workshop looking to improve herself in reading and writing literature as she continues her journey of lifelong learning.

◇◇◇

Esteban Ismael
(83)

Esteban Ismael is a Pushcart-nominated poet and screenwriter from National City. His writing has received recognition from the Helen Zell Writer's Program, the Austin Film Festival, and First Prize in Poetry from *Dogwood: A Journal of Poetry & Prose*. His recent poems can be found in *Southern Humanities Review, Harvard Review, Foundry, Spillway*, and *Conduit*.

◇◇◇

Mary Thorne Kelley
(36, 118)

Mary, an avid reader and conscientious editor for her classmates, has written over 1,000 pages of her autobiography. Raised Victorian-style, she is a trained classical pianist, she was widowed twice, and she has joined several classes since 2007. She continues her writing for the love of it and for class friendships.

◇◇◇

Maria Kotsaftis
(31)

Maria's background is Teutonic on her mother's side, and she hails from Sappho's island of Lesbos on her father's side. A cultural amalgam with both sides vying for supremacy, so far, she sees neither ultimately winning. An ardent lover of literature, she writes creatively.

◇◇◇

Elliott Linwood
(76, 77, 164)

Elliott's aesthetic practices include Life Art: a performance-oriented yet meditative focus toward everyday life. From large-scale sculptural installations to small diaristic haiku, a consistent use of the index is at play in his work—both as interface and signifier—pointing to things which fall within, yet curiously slip beyond various framing devices.

◇◇◇

Rodney Lowman
(8, 62. 124, 136)
Rodney L. Lowman, PhD is President of Lowman & Richardson/Consulting Psychologists and Distinguished Professor Emeritus at CSPP, Alliant International University, San Diego. His latest book is *Career Assessment: Integrating Interests, Abilities, and Personality.* Currently Dr. Lowman edits the "Fundamentals of Consulting Psychology" book series published by the American Psychological Association and co-edits *Diversity Business Review.*

◇◇◇

Elon Mangelson
(91)
Elon, new to the world of workshopping, feels grateful to learn and hone new skills. She lives with her daughter and enjoys her seven children and seventeen grandchildren. She worked in education and real estate and is active in volunteering. She holds a PhD in Sociology and a Masters in Psychology.

◇◇◇

Susheela Narayanan
(18, 116)
A native of India, Susheela has lived in various cities in Canada and the US before making San Diego her current home forty-five years ago. As a trained Montessori educator, she ran several Montessori schools before joining SD Mesa College as a Professor in Child Development. After retirement two years ago, she is returning to her first loves—literature and writing.

◇◇◇

Susan (Susie) L. Parker
(40, 64, 96, 132)
Hometowns have been Falls Church, VA; Virginia Beach, VA; Pensacola, FL; Lake Mary, FL; Tustin, CA. Susan graduated from Tustin High School, before attending Orange Coast Community College; San

Diego State College; University in Hawaii, BA; Lund University in Sweden; University of California, Irvine. Susie likes to write.

◇◇◇

Manuel (Manny) Pia
(4, 128)
Manny, a retired High School Social Science/Language Arts teacher, served 26 years in the U.S. Navy. As a member of the SDCCE Writer's Workshop for two and a half years, he enjoys the association of many writers, poets, and screenplay auteurs. His passions are historical fiction anthologies, short stories, and recently flash fiction.

◇◇◇

Katherine Porter
(37, 51, 88, 157)
Katherine (Kate) Porter, author of *Lessons in Disguise*, works and plays by piecing together words, mosaic tesserae, and cut strips of recycled wool clothing. She writes poetry and fiction, creates mosaic art, and hooks wool rugs. She works as an editor and book formatter while maintaining a rental on Airbnb. Her writer website: TheBookJourneys.com

◇◇◇

Sarah Powers
(60)
Sarah is a California native who relocated from San Francisco to San Diego seven years ago. She loves writing short and flash fiction, baking sourdough raisin bread, playing with her polka-dotted dog, and crocheting cozy hats.

◇◇◇

Frank Primiano
(23, 50, 103)
After retiring from academic and industrial careers that require his writing to be factual, Frank now concentrates on fiction and creative nonfiction. His stories reside in local anthologies and as finalists in several San Diego Book Awards competitions. Frank and his wife, Elaine, are refugees from Cleveland; they now bask in the sun.

◇◇◇

Lindsay Elise Reph
(42)
Lindsay lives in San Diego and enjoys books, the beach, her garden, and twenty nieces and nephews. She's a certified copyeditor, works for a local nonprofit, and is a longtime member of the SDCCE Writer's Workshop. Herein she shares a selection from her book due for publication in 2022, *Grace Comes in Waves*.

◇◇◇

Dave Schmidt
(26, 45, 108, 135)
Dave lives in Mission Hills. After growing up in the Midwest and receiving an advanced degree in Computer Science from a Midwestern university, his current personal goals include writing poetry related to self-help, personal development, and exploring other topics. His work is published in various anthologies.

◇◇◇

Yvonne Sherman
(72)
Yvonne, a second-generation San Diegan, lives a quiet life of retirement with her husband Les in Pacific Beach. The SDCCE Writer's Workshop, expertly guided and taught by the poet, Esteban Ismael, provides Yvonne with a new outlet for artistic expression, and she feels inspired to write a memoir of her exciting and productive life.

◇◇◇

Sandra Sinrud
(1, 168, 179)
Sandra, originally from Chula Vista, lives in San Diego and is a retired editor/document formatter. She primarily writes memoirs and creative nonfiction and hopes to expand out of her comfort zone through Esteban Ismael's Writer's Workshop. Sandra loves writing, photography, her dog Gracie, and her human family and friends.

◇◇◇

Linda Smith
(41, 86, 144)
Originally from Philadelphia, Linda calls San Diego home and that is where her joy of writing was found. Compassion, vulnerability, and humor weave through Linda's poetry and nonfiction stories of family, trauma, and growing up. She was published in an anthology (2014) and excerpts from her teenage diary are in Janet Larson's *My Diary Unlocked* (2014).

◇◇◇

Jean E. Taddonio
(7, 53, 120, 126)
Jean, a native San Diegan and retired hospice nurse, writes poetry and short stories. Faith, encounters with people, nature, and photography inspire her. Jean, author of the children's picture book *The Tale of R-Qu*, has several poems published on websites, in journals, class anthologies, and San Diego Poetry Annuals.

◇◇◇

Nan Valerio
(27, 84, 149)
Nan is from the Midwest but settled in California with her husband following college graduation. After retirement from a career in public and community service, she returns to a favorite pastime of writing to entertain herself, family, friends, and anyone else reading her stories, essays, and memoirs.

◇◇◇

Margaret Wafer
(30)
Margaret is a poet whose work is often gleaned from the love and drama of her large Irish Catholic family. Her poems are published in *San Diego Writers Ink: A Year in Ink*, Volume Nine, and in *The Journal of NAMI California*. She has two self-published chapbooks: *No Shortcuts* and *Firmly in Mid-Air*.

◇◇◇

Hilary Walling
(131)
Hilary is a native Californian, living in San Diego for 48 years. She has attended this SDCCE Writer's Workshop for about seven years. She likes to write memoir, short stories, and occasionally poems for her family and friends.

Lawrence Weiner
(138)
Lawrence, a fiction writer, currently seeks representation and publication of his first novel. Writing stories for all age groups, from picture books through new adult, is the goal he's set for his career. He lives in San Diego where he cofacilitates workshops and attempts to master English, something he imagines may take multiple lives.

Hiedi Woods
(160, 173)
Hiedi has attended the Writer's Workshop since October 2020. She enjoys reading, writing fiction and nonfiction, and editing this anthology. She wrote and edited study guides and playbills for theatre and currently plays with numbers at an investment company. Hiedi holds a BA in English from the University of Connecticut.

Previous Publications

Foley, Nancy:
"Ode to Purple" appeared in the *San Diego Union Tribune*, January 24, 2021

◇◇◇

Ismael, Esteban:
"My Grandmother Dreams" published in *Spillway 24* (2020)

◇◇◇

Porter, Katherine:
"View of Now" inspired by *Luggage Included* a painting by Kyle Denning. Published in *Summation 2019-2020, Ekphrastic Anthology* (edited by Robert O'Sullivan in conjunction with Poets Inland North County and Escondido Arts Partnership Municipal Gallery)

An earlier version of "Here but Gone" was published in *Magic, Mystery, & Murder* (Konstellation Press, 2017). It is a fragment of Kate Porter's upcoming novel and screenplay *Flitter: A Fable of Human Foibles*

◇◇◇

Manufactured by Amazon.ca
Bolton, ON

39580065R00114